THE SERPENT'S TOOTH

A SOLAR COMMONWEALTH NOVELLA

JOHN LALLIER

JCL PRESS

By John Lallier

SOLAR COMMONWEALTH
The Eridani Incident
The Indus Incursion
The Promethean Challenge
The Korhvallan Agenda
The Draconis Campaign
The Pygmalion Plot
The Comae Gambit

TALES of the SOLAR COMMONWEALTH
The Shanghai Strike
The Centauri Betrayal
The Serpent's Tooth

For Tim

AUTHOR'S NOTE

The timeframe for this book begins four years after the events in *The Draconis Campaign*.

As with earlier books in the series, dates and times are provided using multiple calendars and clocks. Since alien worlds as well as human colony planets rotate on their axis and revolve around their suns at different rates from what we know on Earth, they each have their own time keeping system. In general, Terrans continue to use hours, minutes and seconds even if the local day is shorter or longer than 24 hours and measure the local year in local days. Obviously, aliens have developed their own units of measure.

For consistency, Commonwealth Universal Time (CUT), or what we all know today as Greenwich Mean Time, is always included.

"How sharper than a serpent's tooth it is to have a thankless child!"

King Lear (Act 1, Scene 4)

CHAPTER I

Shad-var Swift-Raider Dominator
GC 45217-LAVENDAR-6-1
1582:152:11:06:04 KT (2215JUN20 14:47 CUT)

"Forward again, steerer!" Leeyak-dar ordered as he held the overhead strut to steady himself. Once again, the swift raider altered course as it pulled against its opponent. For the past several minutes, *Dominator* had been locked in a tug-of-war with an alien ship over the prize Leeyak-dar desired: a lander crammed with valuable ore. The fact that the lander belonged to the other ship was of no concern to Dar; like any Krayd, he took what he needed from the universe and woe be to any who stood in his way.

On the screen, the view from *Dominator's* ventral camera laid out the struggle like a sporting event. Two strong cables were pulled taught as the swift raider attempted to wrest away the lander from its former owner. But the Hahntoon hauler was not surrendering its lander, or the beings aboard, without a fight. Invisible traction beams held the smaller craft, pulling it back towards the safety of its home in the larger ship's landing bay.

Leeyak-dar was undeterred. It didn't matter to him that the aliens possessed the more advanced traction beams while his swift raider was limited to grapple lines. Larger Shad-var ships were equipped with traction beams, the thought momentarily returning Leeyak-dar back to the control cabin of *Silver Bounty*. He shook his head to clear the phantasm away and rationalized his predicament: *I always preferred grapple lines!* he fervently reminded himself, dismissing any memories to the contrary. *The physical cables are far more reliable than any invisible tether.* He turned to his right to reinforce that thought.

"Monitor, how do these *peevak* creatures still deny us our prize?" he demanded.

Theelim-arg dared not look back from his station, acutely aware that doing so would draw only further admonishment from the Seventh. Instead, he kept his focus on the screen before him as he made incremental adjustments to the sea of control knobs adjacent. "Their traction projector must differ from that of others, Seventh. Our detectors struggle to identify it for the disrupter."

One of the few unique pieces of tech *Dominator* possessed, the disrupter was taken from a Fugrabth police cruiser orbits before Leeyak-dar's downfall. Since it was never installed on *Silver Bounty*, the former First was free to take it with him into exile as part of his personal property. But of course, there was a very good reason why the device was never made part of his former command – none of his technicians could figure out how to make the damned thing work. Leeyak-dar knew it must work – he'd seen it with his own eyes when the Fugrabth used it to nullify *Silver Bounty's* own traction beams. Fortunately, the strong raider had no difficulty disabling the police cruiser's engines once it broke free of the traction beam, and Leeyak-dar lost no time stripping the alien device from the prize's hull once he extracted knowledge of its function from the surviving prisoners. Sadly, those same prisoners were sold off as slaves before he learned that his examiners were still unable to operate the device. Desperate for any advantage, he had the disrupter mounted on *Dominator* nonetheless, hoping against hope that the technicians here would find more success than those aboard the Shad-var band's leadship. It surprised no one when that proved not to be the case.

Leeyak-dar resisted the urge to rake the vestigial claws of his three-fingered hand across the throat of the monitor, instead encouraging the male to, "Keep trying," as he turned his attention back to the swift raider's pilot. "Reverse pull, Steerer. We will win this battle the old way."

Naymur-elv bent her neck quickly in agreement. "As you say, Seventh," she responded, and she slid her hand along the thrust control plate. On the screen, first one, then the other of the grapple cables became slack before snapping back like bowstrings as the swift raider shifted its position relative to the prized lander. For a brief moment the traction beams from its mothership slipped and the small craft pulled away visibly before the larger ship restored its grasp. Despite this, the standoff quickly resumed with only a minor gain for *Dominator*.

From their new position, Leeyak-dar had a better view of the Hahntoon ship. An ungainly assemblage of orange and lavender boxes sprouting from a central shaft, their adversary displayed nothing like the sleek lines of *Dominator*, the swift raider a clear predator when compared to the other ship's haphazard collection of modules. But one thing was certain – the large hauler had engines to spare as it pulled against the Krayd ship. And just as Leeyak-dar attempted to use the malfunctioning disrupter to break the Hahntoon ship's grasp on the lander, their opponent was using its side guns in an attempt to sever one or both of *Dominator's* cables. Whoever succeeded first would be the victor.

The Seventh squeezed the beam overhead, in part to assure his grip but really as a way to assuage his frustration. The swift raider was a fast attack ship, and yet they were now locked in a battle of engine strength with the hauler. At present, they were too close to the Hahntoon to make use of *Dominator's* forward guns, and their side guns proved ineffective against the alien's shields. Nothing in this situation was playing to the Krayd's strengths.

"Seventh, there is movement," a voice called from across the control cabin. Leeyak-dar turned to see Telrin-vak standing beside the monitor at the detection console.

Dar closed the distance in three long strides (an advantage of being taller than the average Krayd) and demanded, "Bring me good fortune, Overmaster."

Telrin-vak winced at the use of his old title, its use a reminder of all he had lost. Vak did not know whether the Seventh used this appellation to taunt him or to encourage him to work harder to regain all that was taken from him. If the latter, it was not having the desired goal. But as always, the Seventh would not be deterred from his plan. So, the master of *Dominator* focused instead on what he could control. Pointing to the screen mounted high on the bulkhead, he offered, "Three objects rise from the planet. From these values, they will circle to this position."

Leeyak-dar studied the image as the three purple blips grew closer to the green blob that represented *Dominator*. "Projectiles?" he queried with mixed hope, knowing it was unlikely that things would be that simple.

As expected, Telrin-vak ducked his head to the left with a brief shudder. "Too slow, Seventh. And too large. These are most likely fighting craft, sent to aid their hauler."

A sudden change in the path of one of the new intruders seemed to confirm that assertion, as the dotted projection now brought it closer to the Hahntoon hauler while its two partners remained on course to arrive well below the swift raider. To this, Telrin-vak added, "They will reach in one-half *garm-maltee*."

"If they are fight-craft, their guns will reach us before that," Leeyak-dar returned in disgust. He pivoted and yelled across the chamber, "What of the disrupter? Can it be made to function?"

Theelim-arg shuddered and lowered his head in shame. Without turning, he answered in a loud voice, "The proper setting continues to elude. It is unlikely to change in the time allotted."

Leeyak-dar took a deep breath and then, through clenched teeth, he ordered, "Detach the grapple!" Turning his eyes to the forward screen, he continued. "Turn us to face the Hahntoon! Gunner, destroy that lander!" If fate insisted on denying Leeyak-dar his prize, he would make certain that no other had it either.

The young male at the weapons console looked up from his post. Even as the swift raider pivoted to place their adversary in the arc of the main guns of Dominator's mandibles, the screen showed the landing craft being drawn back towards the large hauler. "Seventh, the prize is nearly within their landing hall," he explained.

"Then destroy the landing hall. Destroy the whole damned ship!" Leeyak-dar bellowed.

The gunner jabbed repeatedly at the controls before him. Twin orange beams reached out from *Dominator's* forward pincers to impale the larger ship. Some strikes raked across the doors of the hauler's landing bay, with a few reaching deep into the ship. Flashes of explosion made it difficult to say exactly what those beams struck or even if the gunner was hitting his intended target. So haphazard was his attack that it was possible he wasn't aiming at all. Many of the strikes were scored against the ship's adjacent modules, but these were largely absorbed by the Hahntoon's shields. In all, it was a poor showing.

Lights in the control cabin flickered and purple warning lights flashed. From the detector console, Telrin-vak announced, "The fightcraft are in weapons reach. The protector web holds for now."

The rage that built up in Leeyak-dar ebbed; he was not so far gone that he could not recognize when the game was lost. "Steerer, take us from this place." He squeezed the handrail above him harder. "Take us from this star."

Naymur-elv bent her neck and on the screen the Hahntoon ship slid from view as *Dominator* pivoted and accelerated back out into the depths of space. After a few breaths, she answered, "We cannot leave the system until the grapple lines are drawn in. The cables will foul the sphere drive when it begins to spin."

Leeyak-dar looked with disgust at the ship's master, wondering not for the first time just where Telrin-vak found the swift raider's crew. "Then someone should pull them in," he observed as he moved to the cabin's hatch. "Or I could just sell the bunch of you off to the Ram-dahr!" He threw the hatch open and added, "This raid was a disaster! I will be in my cabin deciding what changes will be made."

The Seventh of the Shad-var band stepped into the corridor beyond the hatch, trying desperately to hold his head high after yet another setback. After more than half an orbit, *Dominator* still had only a handful of minor prizes to show for all his grand plans. *How have I come to this?* he wondered to himself. *And how will I ever return to power at this rate?* Fortunately for Leeyak-dar, there was no one in the corridor to witness his ignoble retreat.

CHAPTER 2

Shad-var Band Hall
Zhev-ga (the Pinnacle), Kray-ssera, Kray-da, Hosh
1581:292:08:02:07 KT (2214OCT19 20:16 CUT)

Leeyak-dar hated the Pinnacle. Despite being the center of power on Kray-da, the capital of their ever-expanding empire, it always reminded Dar of its beginnings. No amount of renovation or modernization could hide the fact that this place began life as an ancient monastery dedicated to a handful of gods to whom he (and many other Krayd) barely paid lip service. If you ignored the recent additions that come with being an interstellar power, it was still just a pile of rocks on a particularly tall mountain.

Indeed, the location was the only benefit to the Pinnacle in Leeyak-dar's opinion as he sniffed the brisk dry mountain air. *At least it lacks the stench of the swamps below*, he thought as he crossed the wide courtyard and entered the hall.

As one of the Eighteen, the Shad-var band was accorded a private structure on the main plaza. Leeyak-dar did not recall which minor deity once adorned this former temple in the past. *Perhaps Golar-bok, the Schemer*, he thought with what a *hooman* might call a smirk, at least within the limits of Dar's firm reptilian skin. *But more likely Perrink-doo, the Nurturer. That would explain much.*

He ignored the hushed whispers as he passed through the lobby and climbed the winding ramp to the third level. A short stretch down the corridor led him to stand before an ornate door; he looked down at the female seated at a station to the right. "I am here to speak with Drayeth-khan," he declared.

The female attender was as old as Leeyak-dar and in no way impressed by either his appearance or his attitude. "Are you summoned by the Chief, Ninth Leeyak-dar?" she purred, seemingly looking down on the male that towered over her. She left no question that this was her domain, and any and all visitors should remember that. The silver adornments in her crests as well as the *triknar* leather vest she wore attested to this fact. She enjoyed the protection of the leader of the Shad-var band and would not be intimidated by any lesser beings than he.

Inwardly fuming, Dar admitted, "I am summoned." This was the real reason he hated visiting the Pinnacle – the fact that he could be dragged here at any moment by the whim of another. But he kept that anger from his voices as he bent his neck. "I ask that he is informed of my compliance."

The old attender eyed Leeyak-dar coldly, reaching for the caller control on her desk before speaking, "The Ninth answers your summons." These words were obviously intended for another, for the attender's attitude softened for a moment before she looked back up to Dar. "You may enter," she informed him with contempt.

Leeyak-dar took a moment to slow his breathing and steel himself before pushing through the ornate portal. Stepping inside, he found a large chamber, though surprisingly not overly large. And very modern. Opposite the door at the far end was a raised dais with an older male perched on an elaborate ... throne. There was no other word for the furnishing, despite how it differed from what any Terran would expect. A heavy metal bench (to favor the Krayd physique) with inlays of silver and copper as well as precious stones. A heavy wooden archway surrounded the seat, similarly adorned.

The throne's occupant was an older Krayd, grown fat around the middle from orbits of life here at the empire's capital. At one time, Drayeth-khan was a formidable male as he rose through the ranks of the band, delivering riches that benefited all. But that time had passed and now he was a symbol of everything that made the Pinnacle abhorrent; a grotesque figure who took more from the band than he contributed, who stuffed his gullet along with the rest of the Eighteen while hard-driving males and females did all the real work.

So focused was Leeyak-dar on his chief that he nearly missed the sight of the First standing to the right of the arched dais. Sselmin-dor held the position Dar lost after that debacle with the *hoomans*. Much as he wanted, Dar found no fault with the male – he saw his opportunity and grabbed for it, bypassing the old guard and quickly sweeping away Leeyak-dar's former choices for Second and Third principals. And since that time, Shad-var's fortunes had grown. Though it galled Dar, Sselmin-dor displayed a gift for squeezing the most of any situation, all to the benefit of the band. And in the end, the band was all. The Krayd had no concept of family or clan as mammals did; once an egg hatched, that individual belong to the band and the band became his or her first and only priority. So as much as it hurt to see another succeed where he had failed, Leeyak-dar knew in his bones that Sselmin-dor was an asset to Shad-var.

"Ninth, you may approach," Drayeth-khan decreed from his throne as the fat old male squirmed in his seat to find a position that did not result in a jolt of pain running down his left leg. Any Krayd with eyes knew why the chief was in such pain: there was too much Khan pressing down on his old joints. Everyone knew this, but no one dared mention it to the male. Such was his reported temper.

As Leeyak-dar drew closer, he was able to make out more details of the older male's attire. A shiny new *triknar* jacket attempted to enclose his girth, no doubt necessitated by the ever-growing circumference. And new adornments were evident along the old male's twin crests, with silver and copper now accounting for more of their surface than the once dark green scales. The sag around the eyes and the drooping jowls gave evidence to Drayeth-khan's advanced age. It would not be long before Shad-var was forced to name a new chief to succeed the current occupant of the office.

When he reached the foot of the dais, Leeyak-dar bent his neck towards the chief, though most would note that the dip was not quite low enough and that he held the position a tad shorter than was customary. Assuming he noticed through his rheumy eyes, Drayeth-khan ignored the slight. "Leeyak-dar, it seems you have survived two orbits as Ninth. Even if your personal style has suffered."

Dar looked down, and while the sapphire leathers of his vest and britches were old, they remained well cared for. That meant the Shad-var chief was referring to the sparse adornments along the Ninth's crests. Where Drayeth-khan sported enough precious metal and gems to finance a small starship, Leeyak-dar was reduced to a pair of cupronickel strips. Indeed, the attender outside the office wore more jewelry. If this was meant to shame Leeyak-dar, it was a weak attempt, and he flexed his elbows in the Krayd equivalent of a shrug. "I adapt to the change in circumstance," he answered.

A gurgle of laughter escaped the chief's crest as he shook his head. "Adapt? More than that, Ninth. You have thrived in your new role. I read the seasonal account books. Our foundries have never been so profitable before; and the gas works over Grahl have doubled their output. I was right to retain you after that ... unfortunate incident. You still have the silver touch." Khan reached into his vest and extracted a small pouch, tossing it casually to his junior principal. "But you should remember to dress the part."

Leeyak-dar snatched the pouch from the air and opened it, pouring the contents into his other hand. Out tumbled a pair of bright copper disks and a pale, greenish gemstone. Dar's lips curled marginally in approval as he placed the items back into the pouch. "A very generous reward," he lied, hoping to hide his disdain for the paltry items. These were nothing compared to the embellishments he once sported.

"It is the least I can do when I ask you to represent Shad-var among the other bands," the chief returned, then peered around the wooden arch to catch the eye of the other male in the chamber. "Don't you agree, First?"

Sselmin-dor bowed his neck to Drayeth-khan as required by tradition before his eyes scanned across the chamber to find their visitor. "Of course. It would hardly do for a Senior of the band to be mistaken for an indigent lieutenant." His tongue flicked out several times to taste the air, while a hand brushed casually against the younger male's fine leather vest. "With a new suit and the proper accessories our chief has already provided, you will once more be presentable, Ninth."

"Seventh," Drayeth-khan corrected, and the head of both younger males snapped up in response to eye the old lizard on his throne. Khan was pleased he was still able to surprise the youngsters who would soon scramble to replace him. One last trick to be played, he mused before he expanded on that revelation. "You have proven you can make our workshops profitable again," Drayeth-khan began, curiously avoiding any glance at the current First for what might be considered an accusation of his prior stewardship. "But that was never where your real talents lay. I need you to bring prizes from outside our current holdings."

With an effort, the old male pushed against the edge of his bench to rise up to a tottering stance on his obviously weakened legs; the noises produced by the strain on the knees were audible across the chamber. Finally erect (or as vertical as an elderly male in poor condition could be expected), Drayeth-khan looked over the crests of Leeyak-dar – no small feat, given that the latter was considerably taller than the average Krayd while Khan barely reached that average even in his youth. "From this moment, you Leeyak-dar are Seventh principal commander of Shad-var. You will be given a ship appropriate to that station." He waved a hand as he rambled, "You may choose from any available of our band for the crew. I expect you to depart as quickly as you can find that crew and return to us with riches from beyond. Do that, and more ships will be placed under your command." The chief wavered, then bounced unceremoniously back onto his bench. Ignoring his near fall, he continued, "You will continue to draw your taste of the foundries and gas works, and you will name your successor as Ninth to oversee those works under your watchful eye. But I want you out in the void, providing for the band again!"

Leeyak-dar was caught off guard, but still managed to steal a furtive glance at his replacement. For the briefest of moments Sselmin-dor allowed his normally placid features to slip and Dar was able to find a mixture of shock and fear in the male's eyes. The First quickly recovered, choosing to focus his attention on Drayeth-khan rather than Shad-var's new Seventh. Before his successor voiced any opposition, Leeyak-dar proclaimed, "You are more than generous, Chief. Rest assured; I will not fail your confidence." He decided against adding "again" – there was no need to remind anyone of an event all were unlikely to forget.

From his throne, Drayeth-khan lowered his heavy brow in amusement before turning again to Sselmin-dor. "First, you will make the necessary arrangements," he commanded.

Sselmin-dor dabbed his head. "Of course, Chief," he replied, then turned to a staffer hitherto shielded from view of the others. "You will see to it," the First advised his lieutenant.

An unassuming female in greyish-blue tanned *chutar* skins stepped forward, wordlessly bending her neck in compliance. For a moment, it was Leeyak-dar who revealed shock and fear at the sight of his former Eyes of the First: Orval-geeth.

Dar looked away quickly, but not quick enough, he was certain. For an instance, their eyes had locked and Leeyak-dar knew that Orval-geeth recognized his confusion. As always, he was unable to read her response.

Shad-var Landing Field
Ryok-dura, Oover-telz, Kray-da, Hosh
1581:301:07:16:08 KT (2214OCT28 19:37 CUT)

Leeyak-dar waited impatiently as the short stream of passengers disembarked the lander and made their way into the transit house. At the tail end of that stream was the male he came to meet – Telrin-vak. The former overmaster of *Silver Bounty* was the first male Dar contacted the moment he returned from the Pinnacle. Leeyak-dar had a new ship and there was only one person he wanted standing in the control cabin. Like Dar, Telrin-vak was discarded after the loss of the Shad-var far-port, reduced to tending to the band's ships in orbit while their real masters were granted time to relax on the planet below between raids. A task normally reserved for the up and coming, not the down and out of favor. Leeyak-dar guessed that the assignment was intended to drive the old male into an early seclusion, but Telrin-vak proved uncooperative. Instead, he took whatever *peevak* assignment he was given and completed it, no doubt to the consternation of his superiors.

Getting along in orbits, Telrin-vak waddled up to Leeyak-dar and bobbed his head in the most minimal gesture of respect. As ever, Leeyak-dar ignored Vak's air of insolence and stretched out his own neck high as if the other male had provided the correct greeting. "Come," he ordered as he moved away from the milling crowds, towards the windows that looked out onto the landing field. Past the glass, a group of slaves was unloading cargo from the lander Vak just arrived aboard; most were Ooverg, the semi-intelligent species native to Kray-da's northern continent. The tall, spindly creatures were conquered centuries ago, after the ignorant almost-animals were caught conspiring with aliens to subjugate the Krayd. For that crime, the Ooverg were made a permanent slave population that existed only to serve the superior Krayd. The docile beasts could be taught simple commands and existed in such numbers that most Krayd barely registered their presence across the Krayd worlds.

The reason the Seventh noticed now was because of a pair of blue-skinned *hoomans* laboring among the Ooverg. That image brought a sneer to Dar's lips. While he never gave any thought to the plight of the Ooverg, the idea of hoomans suffering and serving their masters gave Dar a warm, pleasant feeling. *They deserved all of this and more for what they cost me. The blues and the pinks!* he reasoned.

Eventually, Leeyak-dar returned his attention to Telrin-vak, ordering the shorter male, "Tell me of the ship."

Telrin-vak's tongue whipped out to taste the air before he answered. "It is a ship," he started with little enthusiasm. "The old swift raider *Dominator*. The control cabin has been washed down, as has your cabin, but the stench of a dozen Ooverg still runs through the connectways. They didn't upgrade the guns or the protector, but at least the drive is in fair shape."

Leeyak-dar was too elated by the prospect of returning to space to allow Telrin-vak's evaluation of their new home to dampen his enthusiasm. "We didn't expect them to hand us *Copper Treasure*," he reminded the old master with a glean in his eyes, referring to one of Shad-var's newest and fastest sharp raiders. "At least, not yet." He looked back out the windows, tilting his head up as if to spot *Dominator* as it circled high above the city, "The point is, we have a ship again. The first of many."

"Yes, Seventh," Telrin-vak agreed reluctantly. "Now we just need a crew," he began, then looked apologetically to his commander before explaining, "I've contacted several, but none of our former crewmates is willing to jump ship to join us. It seems most are now fat and well paid on the newer, better ships of the band." Before Leeyak-dar dove into a rant against those who's loyalty faded away as his standing within the band plummeted, the old master added, "But I have found a steerer and a gunner who should do. They're hungry for treasure, as the young usually are."

Leeyak-dar bent his neck subtly in agreement. "Then they will find their fill soon enough. And those who turned away can starve for all I care. We don't need them; let them wallow in their comfortable new lives. The riches will be ours!" Noticing his voice rising at the end, Leeyak-dar looked about to see if any took notice of this outburst. Satisfied that none did, he lowered his voice once more. "And the rest of the crew? We'll need a crafter and some techs for the drive and detectors."

"I have a crafter in mind. One who is also hungry, but not so young; old enough to remember when *Dominator's* drive was new," Vak answered. He paused before explaining, "She'll also be able to get us the techs we need."

"She?" Leeyak-dar asked in surprise. While it was not unheard of for a female to rise beyond the ranks of the techs, it wasn't that common. Leeyak-dar did not recall such a person among the band when he was First.

"She's the best we can get. As I said, no one you remember is willing to ship with us," Telrin-vak reminded the Seventh. "And the young ones wouldn't be able to work a drive this old."

With a flick of his head, Leeyak-dar agreed. "I trust your judgement, Master," he conceded.

Telrin-vak flexed his elbows in response, then reminded his superior, "We still need raiders. Those will be the hardest to convince."

Leeyak-dar curled back his upper lip, revealing an impressive set of sharp yellowed teeth in the Krayd equivalent of a grin. "Have no concern," he insisted as his hand patted the forearm of the master. "I have someone in mind."

CHAPTER 3

Shad-var Instruction Complex
Ryok-dura, Oover-telz, Kray-da, Hosh
1581:302:10:15:01 KT (2214OCT29 23:28 CUT)

The post-mid-light glow from Hosh warmed his face as Leeyak-dar walked up to the low, flat mud-colored building that housed the special training school. A few of the older instructors gave him a perfunctory bob of the head as he passed through the winding corridor on the way to his destination; the younger crowd studiously ignored him. He had no doubt that they all recognized him and expected that reaction of the latter group. His recent advancement by the band's chief would not yet be common knowledge, while his earlier humiliation was all too well known. The newer adults had no desire to catch any of the taint that Leeyak-dar carried.

Finding the desired portal, he yanked at the handle to roll the hatch out of his path. Stepping through, Dar scanned the chamber; the room held a scattering of empty benches arranged in rows, all focused on a single table at the far end of the room. There, a single male sat hunched over peering into some device on the table while occasionally poking the object with one of his stubby claws.

"No one was missing from the last class, which means you are too early for the next one. Leave," a voice boomed out like a rockslide from that lone figure at the table, the head never moving up to acknowledge the intruder.

Leeyak-dar's pulse quickened at the sound of that familiar voice and he strode in defiantly. "I will decide when I am ready to depart, Bolat-ssoo," he returned loudly.

Slowly, the head rose up to reveal an aged face – the weathered hide discolored in places and a deep scar running through the male's left brow with a notch in the blemished skin just above a dead, white eye. The scar continued below the eye until is reached the upper lip, where a noticeable gap left two sharp teeth permanently visible. "I know that voice," Bolat-ssoo admitted with some curiosity as he tilted his head to give his one good eye a chance to identify his visitor.

"You should know my voice, after all the voyages we had on *Silver Bounty*, Raid-master," Leeyak-dar proclaimed as he closed the distance to stop a handful of steps from the instructor's table.

"So gracious of you to visit an old crewmate, Ninth," the big male replied as he pushed against the tabletop to force his body into a mostly upright stance.

Even stooped slightly, Bolat-ssoo was a large Krayd, easily the equal of Leeyak-dar in height and nearly twice as wide. He slowly moved around the table, one hand always hovering over the surface as if ready to plant it for support. As he stepped clear of the furniture, Dar spotted a dull metal framework enclosing Ssoo's right knee, reaching down halfway to his foot while the other end spread up under his cracked *chutar* leather britches. The state of those britches was in stark contrast with the finely oiled vest that struggled to cover Bolat-ssoo's massive chest.

"Seventh," Leeyak-dar corrected his old raid-master, hoping the delay in his rebuke would not alert Bolat-ssoo to his surprise at the male's current condition.

Ssoo stopped and leaned against the table while still beyond Leeyak-dar's reach. "I ask forgiveness, Seventh. It seems I missed the announcement of your elevation." He looked past Dar to the empty chamber beyond. "You must understand; my eye isn't what it once was."

"Then it is fortunate that I am not here looking for a gunner," Leeyak-dar returned, then stood a tad straighter before announcing, "I have a ship and most of a crew, but I need a raid-master. You are my first choice." He paused to gauge Bolat-ssoo's reaction and was disappointed when the old male didn't even flinch. "What do you say? Are you ready to escape this prison?"

Despite the bad knee, Bolat-ssoo didn't waver as he stood rock steady, even as a low gurgling sound began to flow from his crests. This grew in volume for several breaths, but before Leeyak-dar could lash out at the laughter coming from his former underling, Ssoo spoke. "Your first choice? That is unlikely. You must really be desperate to want a half-maimed raid-master for your new ship," he replied in a low even voice with no sign of derision or scorn. "You were never a fool, Seventh. I don't believe you suddenly lost your reason now."

Dar stretched his neck in acknowledgement; he knew Bolat-ssoo would never succumb to base flattery, but he had to try. Best to come clean. "If we were both nine orbits younger, you would of course be my first choice. As it is, you are the only option available to me – you know I can't match the pay of the bigger ships, and the prizes we take in the first orbit's raids will be equally unappealing to any who already have a place in the fleet."

Bolat-ssoo ducked his head down and snorted disapproval from his crest. "Well, we're not nine orbits younger and I can barely walk here from my residence at first-light. I'm in no shape to fight down passageways on some prize ship … assuming your new gunner can cripple one. No, raiding is a young male's game."

"Young raiders aren't the problem," Leeyak-dar countered. "But I need an experienced raid-master to lead them. To train them. Do you really think one of your students could do all that as well as you?"

The stubby claws of Ssoo's hand tapped at the tabletop for a moment before he stopped and swept up the data-plate he was working at earlier. "No. Not one of this batch, though I can find you two or three usable raiders among them," he admitted while he stabbed at the device for a moment. "But I think I have a solution for you. Come with me."

Bolat-ssoo didn't wait for Dar to reply before he lurched past him, quickly crossing the chamber towards the doorway at the rear. The old raid-master was surprisingly fast for someone with only one good leg. Leeyak-dar was forced to lengthen his stride to keep up.

District 17
Ryok-dura, Oover-telz, Kray-da, Hosh
1581:302:11:13:09 KT (2214OCT30 00:41 CUT)

Eleven *garm-maltee* later, Leeyak-dar's groundrunner rolled to a stop in one of the city's seedier warehouse districts. Large conveyors rumbled between the structures, some bringing goods from distant sections of the empire, while others carried these same items away for delivery around the city. Some sported the purple and black colors of Shad-var, though most bore the livery of the other bands that called Ryok-dura home.

"Are you certain you wish to stop here, Seventh," his driver questioned from his perch at the rear of the vehicle.

Leeyak-dar glanced across the cabin to see Bolat-ssoo eyeing him, the old raider almost daring Dar to tell the driver to take them back. Instead, the Seventh stabbed the caller control. "Yes. Remain here until we return." Releasing the control, he waved a hand to direct Bolat-ssoo to precede him to the vehicle's hatch.

Bolat-ssoo sprang the hatch, remarking, "That's what I thought. After all, we've been in tougher settings on eighteen or so raids than any trouble we're likely to find here."

"You were in tougher settings. I was always safe aboard the ship," Dar corrected him as he followed the big Krayd out of the vehicle and stepped into the open, his tongue reflexively flicking out to taste the air. What that detector returned was a harsh, bitter flavor.

A chortle blared from Bolat-ssoo's crest. "You think you were safer on the ship? It may have been warmer, but the big guns were always pointed at you, not us," he commented. His head darted back and forth several times as Ssoo got his bearings, then he swung abruptly to his right while he called out, "This way."

Leeyak-dar was growing weary of the apparent reversal of station between him and Bolat-ssoo, with the latter assuming that the Seventh would simply follow at his bidding. But he gritted his teeth and took the mistreatment in stride (long strides as he hustled to keep up with the surprisingly spry cripple). In the end, it was Dar asking for Ssoo's help – not the other way round.

They walked down a wide alley with buildings on either side, passing workers in the tattered livery of a number of bands, with Shad-var well represented, including a slave-master pressing a clutch of Ooverg to earn their daily meal. The grimy male remained focused on his charges and offered no greeting to the senior members of his band. It was just as well, since Leeyak-dar really wanted no witnesses to this sojourn through the city's underside, lest someone jump to the conclusion that the former Ninth had fallen once more. This thought so distracted him that he nearly collided with Bolat-ssoo when he stopped abruptly in front of one of several nondescript portals.

The building was made of the same mud-brown material as those at the instruction complex, though from the looks of it this one could be several eighteen orbits older. From the cracks in the walls, Leeyak-dar thought it might very well date back to the founding of the city more than a century earlier. The battered sign next to the portal marked the structure a Shad-var property, though the lettering was so marred he was unable to make out any details. Still, Bolat-ssoo seemed convinced they had reached their destination and pressed a claw to the summoner.

After a while a tinny voice screeched out from a grill below the sign. "Closed. Come back next-mark," it whined.

"It's me," Bolat-ssoo growled back with a slight glance at Dar. "Open this, or I'll ram my good foot up your cloaca," he followed with a good-natured bob of the head to his companion.

"Promises, promises," the voice cackled back in disdain, but the angry buzz of an insect preceded the heavy clunk of the portal's latch as the door rolled back to allow them entry.

The pair entered a cavernous, dimly-lit space. Leeyak-dar estimated the structure to be at least three levels high, with numerous crates and containers stacked about on the hard-packed sandy floor. A warehouse of some sort, though what those containers held was a mystery. A scraping sound drew his attention, and he noticed a figure approaching them, the details obscured in silhouette.

"Why are you here?" the same voice as before demanded. "And why is *he* here?" As the small figure stepped into a cone of light from an overhead fixture, Dar was finally able to see their host. An elderly female stopped two *zel-kray* from them, the dingey robe of a Shad-var overworker marking her as a minor member of the band; presumably the one charged with supervising this place.

Bolat-ssoo huffed in response. "You know why I'm here," he growled. "So, tell me: is *he* here?"

The tongue of the female flicked out before she jerked her head to one side. "Yeah. He's here," she admitted, then one hand rose up from the robes, her palm extended upward in the universal sign of expectance. "You know the way."

Bolat-ssoo sneered. "You still owe me. Or did you forget?" He pushed past the smaller Krayd and Leeyak-dar quickly followed, glancing for one last time at the female.

Closing the gap with the old raid-master, Leeyak-dar hissed, "Who was that? And what is this place?"

Bolat-ssoo didn't break stride as he answered. "You don't want to know. Trust me – it will make the denials easier if anyone asks."

Leeyak-dar was growing annoyed at this change in their relationship. Gone was the deference a subordinate should show his superior. After two orbits, Dar was now accustomed to the scorn and glances he received from the lieutenants and masters who were once below him, but this was different. Despite the fact that Leeyak-dar remained a principal commander of the band, Ssoo was treating Dar like a wayward student in one of his classes. Or worse: an equal!

Bolat-ssoo led them through a labyrinth of passages and corridors, around mountains of crates and small nooks secured with the most primitive of locks. Finally, a steep ladder led them to a damp subbasement, their proximity to the harbor evident any time one of the infrequent wall sconces graced them with its minimal illumination. Ample sand scattered along the path did its best to absorb the moisture.

A stout wooden portal blocked their path and Bolat-ssoo shoved it to the side with a grunt. This revealed a large low-ceilinged chamber, the fixtures attached overhead providing slightly greater illumination than in the corridor. Enough to make out several figures milling about on the woven *pleegot* mats that covered the floor. The group ignored the two newcomers, their attention fixed on a brightly lit area towards the far corner. As they grew closer, Leeyak-dar was able to see that the mats ended at a roughly circular depression in the floor. In that depression, a pair of heads bobbed about, the crowd around them moaning and cheering at intervals. When he was within a *zel-kray* of the edge, Dar finally identified what they were fixated on.

Not quite two *zel-kray* below, a rough yellow ring on the hard sandy floor marked the boundaries of a fighting pit. In the center four males were moving about the floor, careful to remain within the yellow circle. None looked more than half Dar's age, and all appeared to be in good physical shape. Each male was armed with a pair of wooden sticks; each stick slightly longer than an adult male's forearm. The polished sheen of the dark blue-grey *muhlat* wood was visible on the upper six-ninths, while the lower three-ninths were wrapped in leather to provide the combatant with a more reliable grip. What he first assumed was a contest between two pairs of fighters quickly revealed itself to be a bout where three of the males were attacking the sole fighter in the center. Dar was about to question this imbalance but stopped when he saw the quick action of the single combatant as he lashed out at his three tormentors with a series of rapid strikes that had all of them reeling back to rethink their strategy.

Leeyak-dar could not look away but demanded of Bolat-ssoo, "Why are we here?" He had seen contests such as this in the public gaming centers of course; even participated a few times as a youngster while he was in advanced school. But those were always single opponent contests, or the occasional demonstration of matched pairs; those fighters wore helmets and were covered in protective padding; the *muhlat* sticks they swung were blunted. Here the fighters wore nothing but a simple pair of cloth britches and their sticks were polished down to form a blade that lacked only a sharp edge. This wasn't a demonstration or a match; this was combat. He knew the rumors that such bouts were held in secret among the lower ranks, but he never dreamed he'd be witness to such a spectacle.

A brassy clang sounded, and a low voice announced, "Two."

In response, the pit fighters found a sudden burst of energy as each sprang forward and a flurry of blows erupted, with the trio finally able to land one or two strikes on their common opponent. But that was nothing compared to the blur of action from their foe, who struck out with blinding speed in every direction, each of his attacks landing on at least one of the tormentors while a few sweeps appeared to strike two or more in succession. And these were not simple blows to the ribs and arms of his attackers but strikes to the face and head that drew splashes of milky white blood from the three.

The gong sounded again, and the voice announced, "One."

The triplets were now breathing heavy and appeared to struggle to deflect the blows coming from the male in the center, who if anything seemed to be moving faster. After a strike to the face, one of the attackers fell back clutching at his short snout as blood flowed freely. The next to go down succumbed to a double sweep of his left leg, and Leeyak-dar thought he heard the distinctive crack of bone as the male tumbled over in agony. The last roared as he threw himself forward, only to have his charge halted when the lone fighter brought his two clubs together to crush both sides of the male's neck, while a kick to the attacker's chest drove him backwards into the wall of the pit and beyond the ragged line of the fighting circle. The fighter with the bloody snout attempted to rise up, but a quick thrust to the back of his head from the soloist rendered the injured contestant motionless.

Even before the final clang, the conqueror stood over his opponents with his eyes darting back and forth to see if any would dare to rise again. Leeyak-dar was astonished – the male didn't even appear to be breathing heavily after all this. He only relaxed when the arbiter ultimately announced, "Victor!" Only then did he appear to acknowledge the cheering crowd that circled the pit with a quick wave of one of his bloodied *muhlat* sticks, then waited at the bottom of the ladder as a pair of elderly males made their way down to tend to his victims. As the winner climbed out of the pit, Bolat-ssoo shoved his way through the crowd, growling at anyone who got in his way.

After a few quick words that Leeyak-dar could not make out, Ssoo led the victorious male to a far corner of the space while he waved Dar to follow. Once they were some distance from the crowd, Bolat-ssoo introduced the younger male, "Seventh, this is Kalgun-dev."

On closer inspection, Dev's appearance suddenly struck Leeyak-dar as somehow familiar, as did the name. "You were very impressive in the pit. I am curious to know why you are down here; I would expect one as skilled as you to compete in the premier tournaments," he offered, trying to remember if that was where he might have seen the younger male before.

Kalgun-dev grunted. "I am no fighter, Seventh. I am a raider!" He threw these words back almost as a challenge.

Bolat-ssoo stepped in quickly, interposing his bulk between them. "Kalgun-dev isn't just *a* raider – he's one of the best I've seen. In fact, he was raid-master on *Tormentor*. You may recall."

Leeyak-dar bent his neck subtly in acknowledgement. He was indeed familiar with *Tormentor*, an older swift raider (though not as old as *Dominator*) that limped back to near port last orbit after a disastrous encounter with an opponent its master had no business challenging; a ship belonging to a new race Krayd-kind had yet to encounter. The fat prize *Tormentor* and its partner, the newer swift raider *Marauder*, hoped to capture turned out to be a trap, the seemingly unarmed cargo hauler suddenly sprouting multiple weapons that wiped out one of the two raiding teams dispatched to capture it. Moments later, a trio of fast-attack ships sprang from behind a nearby gas giant and it suddenly became clear that the two Shad-var raiders were in fact the hunted and not the hunters. Half of *Tormentor's* crew was lost in the battle that followed, including the ship's master, while *Marauder* was obliterated.

The fact that this disastrous encounter came at the insistence of the recently appointed Sixth was quickly obscured to prevent such knowledge from undermining Sselmin-dor. Instead, blame was awkwardly laid at the feet of the conveniently deceased masters, while the few surviving senior staff of *Tormentor* was similarly smeared for this fiasco. That was why Kalgun-dev's name was familiar to Leeyak-dar, but it didn't explain why he *looked* familiar – the report Dar perused on this matter contained no images of the minor players, only the two masters.

The Seventh eyed the younger male silently before admitting, "It changes nothing, but you were mistreated by your senior. Just as your master was fortunate to extract *Tormentor* from that ambush, you showed skill avoiding the vermin's weapons and bringing your lander back to the raider while your partner was destroyed. You should have been rewarded ... but that decision was not mine to make."

Kalgun-dev flexed his elbows in a shrug. "That is the past; it cannot be changed," he remarked, then flicked his head towards Ssoo. "The raid-master says you have a ship. That you are looking for a crew," he began, then folded his arms across his broad chest. "Can you afford to add a raider who had been anointed a coward and a fool by the First?"

Leeyak-dar smirked, leaning back to bring himself to his full height as he matched Kalgun-dev's stance, his eyes level with the top of Dev's crests. "You know my story as well as I know yours. If you will follow a senior who had fallen even further, I will name you raid-master of *Dominator*."

The younger male thought for a moment, then dropped his arms to his side, then stretched out his neck and shook his head. "Where you lead, I follow; what you require, I take for you, Seventh," Kalgun-dev agreed.

CHAPTER 4

Shad-var Building, District 2
Ryok-dura, Oover-telz, Kray-da, Hosh
1581:304:06:08:06 KT (2214OCT31 17:43 CUT)

Like the four other great bands that shared the city of Ryok-dura, the Shad-var compound sat on one of the hills that surrounded the lower harbor district. These compounds housed the main offices and residences of each band's leading members, giving those privileged few an unencumbered view of their holdings and operations below. Even before his fall from First principal, Leeyak-dar avoided the petty palace of the Shad-var, preferring to stay aboard *Silver Bounty* whenever possible. When he was forced to remain planet side, as he had for the past two orbits as Ninth, he worked from the band's old offices in the city's core.

The offices of Seventh were only a minor step up from his previous location on the level below, but it hardly mattered to Leeyak-dar. He had a ship now and planned to spend as little time as possible in this new nest. Indeed, he was here this morning to ensure that all was in place to permit him a timely exit from the Hosh system.

He marched through the first level lobby and into the ascender before anyone waylaid him for whatever inconsequential matter each might have that he or she believed required the Seventh's immediate attention. As the platform rose to the fourth level, Dar experienced a slight nostalgia for his previous position – it was so much easier to enter the building undisturbed when most of the other occupants were studiously avoiding him.

He resumed his earlier pace as he moved from the ascender to the portal of his office, ignoring the attender parked nearby as she rose to greet him. If she said anything, it was lost to the sound of the portal closing firmly behind him.

"Seventh," a more familiar voice stopped Leeyak-dar in his tracks just short of his desk. He turned to find his Voice already loitering in the office. Shurvil-maj was a recent acquisition; she joined his crew half an orbit ago but was already proving herself indispensable. A sharp eye and a sharp mind, she might be vying for a spot among the numbered commanders in nine orbits if it weren't for one unfortunate setback: she was a female. Dar would have named her the new Ninth otherwise, but that honor was destined to fall to one less qualified. The best Leeyak-dar could do was make her his first lieutenant, his Voice authorized to speak for him in all matters.

Shurvil-maj stood there waiting, a vision in teal-blue *chutar* vest and britches that highlighted her youth and energy, the color complimenting the deep green of her head scales while contrasting with the ivory coloring at the base of her neck. But most noticeable were her dusky red eyes, a feature that set her apart from the majority of Krayd with their simple black eyes. Not for the first time, Dar experienced rumblings in his cloaca at the sight of her, but quickly pushed such animal urges aside. This female was far too valuable to be used for simple rutting. She took care of a much more important need of his – business! Acquiring wealth for the band to hasten his rise back to real power.

"You wasted no time relocating us to the new space, I see," he commented as he moved to stand behind the large desk, its cold polished stone top a reasonable upgrade over the dull wooden surface he used one level below. His upper lip curled back on one side briefly. "You should be quite comfortable in here while I'm away."

Retrieving a data-plate from the low table, she answered, "This office must reflect your new status to all who are summoned. Even in your absence."

Leeyak-dar knew that Shurvil-maj did not agree with his decision to depart aboard *Dominator* for the swift raider's first runs. She was quite vocal in her belief that it was important for the new Seventh to be seen about Ryok-dura in his new position so soon after the promotion, not to scamper off and leave underlings to keep things running smoothly. In fact, she was more vocal than other commanders would have permitted, including Leeyak-dar when he was First. But Dar had learned a lesson from his demotion; he needed to hear opposing views, even if he didn't like it. Perhaps if he had, he might have avoided the problems that led to his demotion in the first place.

Still, he wasn't budging in this instance. "It is unavoidable. I must see how this new crew performs. The Chief is looking for treasure, and we won't be here very long if we don't deliver. There will be time later to preen about for the gawkers."

Maj bent her neck, more in acceptance than agreement. "They better perform; they are costing us enough," she tossed back. "You were very generous with their contracts. Especially considering their prior experience ... or should I say lack of experience."

Dar flexed his elbows as he settled on his new bench, the stiff padding already conforming to the shape of his hind. *Maybe Maj is correct, and I should stay here for a nine-mark*, he mused. "You know we cannot sign a better, more experienced crew. We don't have the reputation or the funds," he responded.

"Then why are you paying them more than they're worth?" Maj demanded.

Leeyak-dar leaned forward, his palms planted on the stone top of the desk. "Because I have to make them believe that they are worthy, if I expect them to perform like a crew that's already proven itself. If I pay them like fourth-ranked pretenders, that's all they'll ever be!"

Shurvil-maj was not convinced. "You could have rewarded them after they took their first prize," she countered.

Dar leaned back again. "Telrin-vak said much the same. It's worked in the past ... sometimes; and sometimes it doesn't work. I don't have the luxury of time to see what that produces later; we need results now."

Maj glanced at her data-plate. "We must hope that our new master has not forgotten how to raid after so long an absence," Maj remarked.

Leeyak-dar gurgled in amusement. "Do not fear. The old lizard still remembers which end of the ship brings death, and where to secure the loot. And with what we're paying the crew, there will be no shares of what we take. It will all come back here."

"Good," Shurvil-maj relented, then moved to her next topic. "I don't have the same level of trust that you have in the new Ninth. If he begins nipping at the foundries' profits, you will have a hard time making these payments to your new crew."

Truth be told, Leeyak-dar did not trust his successor, but for a different reason. After the band suffered a series of setbacks (not all laid at the feet of their former First), the candidates for Ninth were not all that many. The male Dar ended up choosing was a middling producer at best; he was less concerned with Rolehn-dru dipping his snout in the profits than he was that the uninspiring male would simply fail to make any profit. His fingers drummed on the stone desktop as he explained, "That is why I need you here. To ... keep your eye on our new colleague and assess the situation. If needed, remind him of my requirements."

"And if he fails to heed my advice," Shurvil-maj pressed.

"Then he is ignoring my demands," Leeyak-dar answered firmly. He stood, leaning forward with both hands firmly planted on the desktop. "You are my Voice; when you speak, it is as me. I will remind Rolehn-dru of this fact. If he does choose to challenge my Voice, you can take whatever action you need to correct the situation. And I will have his head when I return." He sat back on his bench before adding, "I will remind him of that fact as well."

Shurvil-maj tilted her head back and shook it in a sign of agreement. "I will do all I can to expand your holdings, Seventh," she declared. She moved towards the portal, saying, "If there is nothing more you require, I must meet with the attender I assigned to our new Ninth. I will let her know of your wishes."

"Go," Leeyak-dar agreed with the flick of his hand, dismissing his Voice to tend to such matters while he pulled his data-plate from a shelf under his desk. With a series of taps, he brought up the crew list and manifest of *Dominator* for one last review. He would speak with Rolehn-dru later; the male deserved at least a warning of what was to come if he crossed Shurvil-maj.

Waystation 2
GC 43291-CYAN-1 (Hosh), Kray-da orbit
1581:305:09:05:03 KT (2215NOV01 21:17 CUT)

Leeyak-dar stared at the large forward window of the bubble skiff as the steerer brought the fragile craft about in a gentle arc around an old Vor-thal hauler; once clear of the minor band's ship, Dar was finally able to spot their destination. *Dominator* was just as Telrin-vak described it – an old swift raider, well past its prime. The greenish hull was marred by patches and scorch marks from eighteens of repairs over the past 140 orbits. The left-side weapons mandible appeared canted downwards when compared to the one on the right, and it was obvious that one of the side guns was disabled or possibly missing. The drive spheres also looked like they had seen better rotations, though Vak assured him earlier that all drive systems were working. He would soon find out if the master was correct.

The skiff pivoted as it approached the raider's rear flank and eased into the ship's cargo hold. It took a moment for the outer portal to close and for the chamber to fill with air. Once it did, Leeyak-dar bounded out of the simple craft and was finally able to stand on the deck of his new leadship! The moment might have been more impressive if he wasn't greeted by the screech of the inner portal as it rolled back to allow egress.

"Damn you, Elldor-min! Get one of your crafters to fix that!" Telrin-vak bellowed as he crossed into the cargo hold. He stopped a respectful distance from Leeyak-dar and ducked his head low. "Seventh, be welcome in *Dominator*!" he proudly proclaimed.

Leeyak-dar snapped his jaw. "It is good to feel deck-metal beneath my pads once more," he answered with enthusiasm. Nothing would dampen this moment. He flicked his head to the two standing behind the ship's master.

Telrin-vak twisted about and gestured to his two lieutenants, "You already know our raid-master, Kalgun-dev. And this one is Elldor-min, the drive-master," the old male declared.

Kalgun-dev ducked his head appropriately, while the female next to him seemed to participate grudgingly. She was short, even for a female, and stout. The mottled leathery skin of Elldor-min's face and hands spoke to the many orbits she had seen in her life; far more than Leeyak-dar could claim and probably more than Telrin-vak had witnessed. In contrast, the fresh patina of her orange *gellrehk* leather coverings revealed the uniform to be brand new; the outfit had none of the shiny, worn joints one might expect from a crafter of such advanced orbits. It was obvious that this female would be more comfortable in the basic cloth coverall of her underlings, a well-worn outfit with frayed ends and splatters of grease after so many *garm-liktee* spent in the bowels of the ship, repairing some malfunctioning device or another. Standing in front of the Seventh, Elldor-min kept her leathery face down, never looking Leeyak-dar in the eyes as her feet appeared to perform a nervous dance of their own design.

"We are well served. I am certain that you will both bring treasures to Shad-var," the Seventh replied. The raid-master had no need of reassurance from Leeyak-dar, so the Seventh turned his attention to Elldor-min. "I am counting on you to keep this old swift raider running. It is my hope that it has a few good raids left in it. Though from what I saw as I approached, the orbits have not been gentle to it."

A snort of derision sounded from the female's crest, which quickly transformed into a coughing jag. When she recovered, she answered, "Have no concern, Seventh. *Dominator* still had legs to run ... and a few teeth that will yet bite into your adversary's hide. He will not fail you in your quest."

Dar twisted his head. It was not uncommon for a crafter to refer to his or her ship as 'he' rather than 'it'; the trade often assumed a bond with their charge that other members of the crew did not. "See that he doesn't," Leeyak-dar advised, then looked back to Telrin-vak. "Well, Master? Are we ready to go forward?"

Telrin-vak bent his neck, then gestured to the inner portal, "We await your order, Seventh."

Leeyak-dar preceded his master and crew into the long connectway that ran from the bulbous forward main module to the cramp drive control cabin at the rear of the ship. As his eyes followed the trio who greeted him at the skiff, another form was added to the party – a worker in basic Shad-var kit struggled to keep up as he hefted Leeyak-dar's travel chest. Dar glanced at Telrin-vak, "Have we no slaves, Master?"

Dominator's captain shrugged. "None could be spared from your other works, Seventh. It is a minor matter; your Voice promises we will be supplied in time for our first raid."

Leeyak-dar could not argue with Shurvil-maj's reasoning – there was little for a slave to do for the few rotations Dominator would be journeying this time. And in her mind, it kept costs down and profits up. Always a worthy goal. Still, he was surprised he was not informed on this decision and made a note to review all communications between the master and his senior staff.

A few of the lights in the connectway flickered while others seemed overly bright when compared with others in the line. It was clear that the crafters were doing their best to bring the old hull up to Shad-var standards, but orbits of neglect were not erased in a rotation. A part of Leeyak-dar found it poetic that he should be given Dominator in this state; no small part of that neglect occurred while he was First. It was fitting that he be the one to finally address his handiwork.

For such a small ship, it took longer to reach their destination than Dar would have imagined. At last, the hatch to the command cabin opened before them and the quartet stepped inside (the worker silently disappeared at some earlier juncture without drawing the Seventh's attention, much to his credit).

Like the rest of the ship, the nerve center of Dominator showed its age. The typical three post arrangement for the gunner, master and steerer occupied the center of the cabin towards the front, though the benches looked thread-bare, and the supporting structure was stripped down to its basic framework. When an overly young male leapt up from the master's position, Leeyak-dar didn't even have time to comment that the individual looked too young for the position he occupied. Instead, his thoughts focused more on what wasn't there than what was. Where the large main screen was expected, an empty mounting bracket stood testament to its absence.

Leeyak-dar extended an arm to the missing screen and called out to the small figure seated at the helm station. "Steerer, how do you plan to guide us when you cannot see where we are going?" he demanded.

The target of his question jumped out of the chair and turned to face the Seventh. Once upright, Leeyak-dar saw that it was yet another female, this one slightly taller than the drive-master and about half her age. "Commander, we must rely on these," the youngling responded, gesturing to the visor that rested just below her short crest. With a hand, she lowered the device, obscuring her bright black eyes behind its solid surface.

"Again, a temporary solution, Seventh," Telrin-vak explained. "At least, until the replacement for the main screen is delivered in a nine-mark. The circuitry in the original could not be mended and we were forced to remove it."

Leeyak-dar ducked his head to one side and snorted in frustration, then strode across the cabin to an empty space away from the rest of the crew. Vak hurried to join him. Dar lowered his head and demanded in hush tones, "Master, I need the truth! Is this raider truly space worthy? Has the First pulled some trick here?"

Telrin-vak never wavered. "Seventh, the ship is functional ... but just. I have no doubt the First was unable to find an older, more worn ship in the Shad-var inventory. But if he really wanted to sabotage you, he would have purchased a discarded hull from the Trel-not or some other useless band. What he gave you was the worst ship we have. But we were not expecting *Silver Bounty* as you said before. We can make *Dominator* whole again, but it will take time." He glanced over his shoulder to the others studiously avoiding his gaze from the other side of the cabin. "The crew is ready to do this for you. They are new, but they will soon be as feared as any ship of the band. They only need your command to make it so."

"I will hold you to that, Master," Leeyak-dar promised as he peered over Vak's crests at the collection of children and the aged. With a snap of his jaw, he raised his voice. "Very well. Let us see just what our new swift raider can do!" He was rewarded with enthusiastic looks from the assembled crew of Dominator. Leeyak-dar snapped his jaw once more in response. He was feeling better now about his decision to invest so much into this inexperienced group as he saw them return to their tasks to make the ship ready. *This is going to work*, he mused. After all, with Dar and Telrin-vak to lead them, what could go wrong.

CHAPTER 5

Shad-var Tower, District 38
Ryok-dura, Oover-telz, Kray-da, Hosh
1582:160:10:07:10 KT (2215JUN28 13:14 CUT)

Sselmin-dor stood in his tower office before the floor-to-ceiling transparent wall that looked out over the city below and the deep green harbor beyond, gently rocking back and forth on his heels to the apparent rhythm of the waves sweeping in from the vast ocean past the breakers. While Shad-var's tower was not as grand as the one at the center of the Cho-peg compound on the highest of the five hills, the Shad-var building was actually taller, with two extra levels that brought it nearly even with the Cho-peg spire, despite starting from a lower base. Sselmin-dor would sometimes venture to the facing chamber and salute the First of Cho-peg as he toiled in his office. A reminder to his rival to watch his back; Shad-var was advancing.

But this rotation he chose to stand in his own office, watching the whitecaps as they washed into the numerous docks below while others simply dissolved into the pale green shallows that wrapped around the undeveloped outer shore. Dor found the steady beat mesmerizing and calming, and it made him think of his stewardship of the band. He was a firm believer in no grand schemes, no reckless endeavors; progress was made by the slow, steady advancement that took Shad-var ever higher. Unlike his predecessor, he had no intention of risking it all on one daring throw of the stones for some improbable payoff. After all, how did all that turn out for Leeyak-dar?

Unlike Leeyak-dar, Sselmin-dor was far more comfortable in this office than he was in the control cabin of the band's lead-ship. Each orbit, he would attend to one or two raids – mostly to remind the lesser commanders and ship masters that their First was keeping an eye on them. But he much preferred managing the affairs of the band from this tower. The feel of the moss-like carpet under pads of his feet was preferable to the constant thrum of a raider's engines vibrating the deck plates.

Absorbed by these thoughts, Sselmin-dor was startled when the voice of his Eyes interrupted him. "First, there is a dispatch you should review," Orval-geeth informed him. She stood just inside the doorway, always careful to announce her presence when the First was deep in thought. It would not do to arouse any suspicion that she might be spying on her superior when he was otherwise occupied. Of course, if Orval-geeth truly were spying on Sselmin-dor, she knew of at least nine ways to prevent anyone from discovering that fact.

The First moved to the onyx-covered desk and picked up his data-plate. A flashing glyph caught his attention, and he tapped it with his center claw. A splash of text provided the highlights (or more accurately lowlights) of the latest actions of Shad-var's Seventh as he led the swift raider *Dominator* once again on a fruitless exercise. If each such attempt was not costing the band much needed currency, the futility of the action would be amusing. Instead, he flicked a symbol at the bottom of the dispatch and the text was replaced with a table of figures outlining the expenses incurred by this latest misadventure. Another tap, and he compared those figures to the other Shad-var operations under Leeyak-dar's control. Sadly, the two numbers were uncomfortably similar – the Seventh's little adventure was undoing whatever good he was providing the band. And that was before Sselmin-dor included all of the upfront costs needed to make the old swift raider a viable threat to its victims. In disgust, he tossed the plate back on the desktop.

"A problem, First?" Orval-geeth inquired gently.

Sselmin-dor twisted his head in a quizzical fashion. "You are my eyes. You already know that there is a problem," the First tossed back, then planted himself on his bench behind the desk, reaching to retrieve the device he just discarded. "I know him – Leeyak-dar will blame these failures on the ship he was given, and the Chief will question why I would punish his favorite commander."

"But you did not punish the Seventh," Orval-geeth protested. "*Dominator* was the only ship available; *Annihilator* still remains at the mender station, unable to make use of its sphere drive. The Chief cannot expect you to divert one of the newer ships away from its successful raids just to satisfy the Seventh's need to impress."

Sselmin-dor uncharacteristically snapped his jaw before insisting, "The Chief is not interested in petty machinations; he expects treasure to flow into our vaults in excess of the cost of acquiring it. He really doesn't care how that is achieved. And he will not bother checking to see who is at fault – I am the First and it becomes my responsibility." He slapped a hand on the desktop, the vestigial claws of his hand leaving the hard surface unmarred. Eons back, his ancestors would have left deep gouges in stone ... but then again, they had no use for desktops or starships. Simpler times.

Orval-geeth was not so certain. "Leeyak-dar failed the Chief before and was reduced. The Chief will see that this latest failure is entirely of his making. You did not select the crew the Seventh employs; you did not select the targets that he has failed to capture," she argued.

Dor flexed his elbows in frustration. "Do you not hear my words? Our Chief has a fondness for Leeyak-dar that blinds him to the male's flaws. He was reduced from First because there was no other option – the First must bear the cost of failure. That is a rule even a Chief cannot ignore. But Leeyak-dar remained a commander, albeit of the lowest kind. Any other First would be lucky to be left as master of a cargo hauler," Sselmin-dor declared. After a breath, he looked up at the ceiling, a canopy of aromatic leaves providing a soothing contrast to the offices of lesser members of the band. "You have given me valuable advice since becoming my Eyes, Orval-geeth. But on this, you must accept my interpretation. I have spoken extensively with the Chief and know his mind."

Recognizing that she would not sway her First on this point, Orval-geeth pivoted. "Then what should be done? How can we correct the situation?"

Dor continued to look to the leaves above him, as if he expected sunlight to suddenly pierce the blanket above him. "We must hope that Leeyak-dar finally finds a target that his inept crew can capture. Either that, or that the next ship they approach does us a favor and kills the Seventh in retaliation," he explained. His voice gave no indication of which solution he preferred.

Orval-geeth bent her neck in acknowledgement of the First words. Though studious to avoid showing any preference, Geeth knew exactly what outcome she would work towards.

District 12
Ryok-dura, Oover-telz, Kray-da, Hosh
1582:163:16:03:13 KT (2215JUL01 20:49 CUT)

Despite the time she spent in the Shad-var compound high above the city, Orval-geeth was perfectly at ease walking through the lower wards, where the common workers and techs far outnumbered the commanders and their lieutenants. When she served Leeyak-dar, she and her *brother* (she still stumbled over the Ooverg concept, so alien to her species) would often wander out into the early evening to share a meal among the lower ranks of their band, allowing Geeth to keep an aural membrane to any grumblings that might present a future issue for the First.

Since joining Sselmin-dor's retinue, such visits were less frequent. Not just because Orval-brak was gone, but because the new First found such clandestine information gathering ineffective. He believed his more conservative administration of the band's operations were less likely to be threatened by dissent among the lower ranks than by scheming among the upper echelon. So far, his evaluation was proving correct, and Orval-geeth only came down to the lower districts once a nine-mark for the past orbit. When she did, her arrival was out in the open for all to see the Eyes of the First as she inspected the band's holdings.

Such was not the case this evening. Gone were the fine leathers she wore in the tower; instead, she was covered in a basic worker's outfit sporting the muted caramel & fern colors of the Gul-zir band, a minor group eking out an existence on the large northern continent. Even though she was unlikely to encounter a true member of that band this evening, she clutched a tattered grey cloak around herself to limit the number of observers as well as to ward off the chill in the air.

With Hosh already set below the horizon, the only light that broke the darkness came from the infrequent illuminator staffs the governing bands grudgingly provided to this derelict district. Most of the buildings down here were storage depots or workshops, locked tight for the night. No light came from the few windows along those structures.

Orval-geeth approached one of the few exceptions – a grimy translucent portal that barely stood out from all the blackened doorways she already passed. With a hearty shove, she pushed the entrance open. Her reward was access to a chamber only slightly brighter than the evening outside. A flick of her tongue returned the rancid smells of meat well past its serving time, and a mixture of fruit alcohol and bile that caused her to wonder if the liquid had been regurgitated to mask the smell of the meat. As often was the case, she made a mental note to consume nothing in this particular establishment.

Squeezing past an assortment of low-level workers availing themselves of the tavern's questionable fare, Geeth eventually reached an empty bench among the tables along the back wall. She remained silent and squatted on the rickety seat, leaning on the table to avoid the chance that even her minimal mass could somehow cause the bench to splinter.

"You're late," the female across from her mumbled; the timber in her voices the only indicator of her gender. She was dressed much like Orval-Geeth, with a dark cloak obscuring a mustard and teal work suit; Geeth did not recall which band bore those colors. Also, like Geeth, the female was hunched down, her muzzle carefully avoiding contact with the bowl of oily broth placed before her. Just another nobody in a sea of nobodies. The only thing that set her apart were her eyes; while most Krayd, including Orval-Geeth, had black eyes, this shadowy figure's eyes were instead a deep shade of dark grey. Not nearly as rare as red eyes, but still a mark that set her apart from the majority of her kind.

"It couldn't be helped; your message came late in the rotation," Orval-Geeth tossed back.

The female flicked her tongue to one side, avoiding the gruel in front of her. After a moment she brought her head up briefly. "I have what you're looking for. But the price has gone up ... two ninths."

Orval-geeth was careful not to react, either physically or verbally, to the all too expected attempt to renegotiate. Instead, she flicked her own tongue out, letting it hang in the air a tad too long for polite company. "No. We had an agreement, and I expect you to honor your bond."

Her companion was quiet for a moment, then shoved the bowl to the center of the table. "This didn't come cheap, and I have to cover my expenses. If you're no longer interested, I can always find another buyer," the female threatened.

Orval-geeth sat back a fraction, her hands gripping the edge of the table as her claws began to dig into the uneven surface, weakened over time by numerous spills. With the bob of her head she countered, "One ninth, for your exorbitant expenses. But no more; or you will never do business with Shad-var or our allies again." Leaning forward, she hissed, "Decide now."

It took only the blink of an eye for the female in mustard to stretch out her neck. "Agreed," she said, reaching into a pocket to extract a wafer of heavy paper. She passed this cautiously to Geeth. "Be at this address next-mark at 17. And bring silver, no gems. I'm not bringing an evaluator to let all the worlds know about our little transaction."

Orval-geeth accepted the paper, glancing at the symbols scrawled across it in an uneven hand. "Very well. My representative will be carrying this wafer for confirmation," Geeth noted as she held the card up before secreting it to an unseen compartment in her tunic. "Plus, your silver; no gems," she added. The Eyes of the First had no trouble agreeing to that point. The device the female refused to carry would be needed to verify the purity of any gemstones and to provide their current value. But to do so, it would need to wirelessly access the central exchange. Like her reticent partner, Orval-geeth had no desire to have any trace of this trade available to the prying eyes of her competitors.

With their business concluded, Orval-geeth pushed herself up from the bench. She had no desire to spend another *garm-voshtee* in this house of vermin. She was about to turn away when her host called out.

"A pleasure doing business. As always," the other female declared, a little too loudly for Geeth's tastes.

In response the Eyes of the First hissed, "That will be decided when I see what my silver has purchased. If I am not satisfied, it will be the last business you ever do."

The other female swallowed but said nothing in response, allowing that warning to hang in the air as Orval-geeth disappeared into the night.

Shad-var Swift-Raider Dominator
GC 43927-INDIGO-9-6, Krayd Near-port
1582:166:09:02:08 KT (2215JUL04 11:17 CUT)

His cabin within the main hull of *Dominator* was far smaller than the space he called home on *Silver Bounty* for so many orbits, with few of the amenities he once enjoyed. Still, Leeyak-dar found it preferable to his more spacious quarters in Ryok-dura. Even now, circling the minor moon that housed Near-port, the gentle vibration of the deck plates reminded Dar that he was on a ship, which was where he truly belonged.

He tore a strip of flesh from the block of meat in his feed-bowl and tilted his head back to allow it to drop down his throat. Even ship's rations seemed more satisfying than the finer fare available to him in the city. *I can have any meal I want on Kray-da and still I would choose this. Truly, I was hatched to fly!* he reveled silently, not for the first time. *Now if only I can whip this crew into shape!*

The ship arrived three rotations ago with little to show for five nine-marks of raiding. What little treasure *Dominator* carried only partially paid for the fuel and provisions it took on here. If their luck did not change soon, Leeyak-dar would have no choice but to return to the home world in disgrace. Even with the support of the Chief, Sselmin-dor would not allow the Seventh to squander the band's wealth indefinitely.

The buzz from the cabin's hatch interrupted these thoughts. With a grunt, Leeyak-dar dropped the bowl on the small table and stalked over to slap an angry hand at the hatch control. It rolled away to reveal Telrin-vak standing stiffly in the connectway, his eyes cast down.

"It is mid-light, Master. I assume you have good cause for disturbing my feeding," the Seventh challenged. He took a step back and bade the other male forward. "Enter if you must."

Telrin-vak bent his head low as he entered, then moved to an empty corner in the cramped cabin, hoping to disturb his commander as little as possible. "Forgiveness, Seventh. The caller received a message from home."

Leeyak-dar swallowed another strip of meat and tossed the bowl aside. "What of it? Does our First demand yet another accounting of our actions?" he scoffed.

The old master flexed his arms. "I cannot say, Seventh. The message is for you alone; the monitor has already delivered it for your review," he confessed, his eyes flicking to the data-plate sitting on the edge of the cabin's sleep nest.

Leeyak-dar sighed and followed the master's gaze, rescuing the device from the artificial sand pit and activating it with a graze of his claw. As the screen brightened, a glaring purple symbol flashed into view. Dar flicked his tongue at the receptor recessed into the bulbous edge of the plate and waited. Inside, the discriminator broke down the sample he provided and extracted the Seventh's genetic code. This was then used as a key to decipher the encrypted message; with a gentle blurp, the purple symbol disappeared from the data-plate's screen and was replaced with a block of text.

The Seventh's eyes quickly consumed the revealed message and once satisfied, he flicked a control to remove the text and scrub all evidence of its contents from the system. With a slight sneer he said,

"It appears Shivee-gop, the Gamer, has finally decided to grace us with his favor." Though Leeyak-dar had no use for any of the ancient deities of his people, he found the legends of the old trickster the entertaining, and occasionally invoked his name. Dar shook the data-plate in the air before tossing it onto his pseudo-sandy bed. "My Voice has found a trophy for us. One that could make this long draught a distant memory."

Telrin-vak tilted his head. "Really? What is it?" he asked.

Leeyak-dar shrugged. "She does not include the details, lest one of our rivals would intercept it. We will learn all we need when we meet."

The old master was wary of the Seventh's new favored advisor, questioning her rapid rise in power, though he would never voice those concerns to Leeyak-dar. In most things, Telrin-vak lived by a simple adage: if anything seemed too good to be true, keep clear. He put no stock in relying on superstition; never one to implore the intervention of the Gamer or the Schemer. Good luck or bad was simply a matter of chance, and no one controlled that.

Leeyak-dar would agree with most of that, but he also never questioned good fortune. No matter the source, you grabbed opportunity and never let is escape. "We will travel to Garr-sum."

Now Telrin-vak was stunned, and openly questioned the plan. "Why? The band has no holdings there; no agents," he blurted out. Aside from the obligatory office here at Near-port and the other at Mid-port, all of Shad-var's operations beyond the home system were on Trogok, the Krayd's oldest and largest captured world. The band had nothing of value on the world Leeyak-dar just named.

The Seventh stared at the ship's master in surprise, the lids of his eyes half closing until his bulbous black eyes were reduced to two vertical slits. "We go because the information we seek is there. For a worthy prize, we would go to the galaxy's core and beyond."

After some quick calculations in his head, Telrin-vak pressed, "It is more than thirty rotations travel to Garr-sum ... in the wrong direction. There is nothing nearby we would value."

Leeyak-dar grew angry with the older male. "Forgive me, Master. I was unaware we were blessed with greater opportunities so close to Near-port. Please, enlighten me. What great bounty awaits us a mere handful of rotations from this spot?" he demanded. He waited a moment, his breathing heavy as Telrin-vak stood frozen before him. "You forget yourself, Master. I command here! I decide where we go, and when we go! Not you!" he bellowed.

Telrin-vak swallowed any retort he thought to make, and bent his neck low without a sound in. His only option was obedience now.

Satisfied that the master would remember this moment, Leeyak-dar softened his tone. "Our supplies are whole again. Recall the crew," he ordered. While Dar was content to spend his rotations aboard *Dominator*, most of the crew did not share his opinion. Many were now availing themselves of the various taverns and gaming dens of Near-port. An expensive yet necessary respite after spending several nine-marks in deep space. "We will depart for Garr-sum at mid-dark."

Telrin-vak bobbed his head, answering in neutral voices, "It will be as you say, Seventh."

Leeyak-dar stretched his neck upward as much as the low ceiling of the cabin would allow and shook his head, trying to cajole his old raiding companion. "Come now, Vak. We've never been to Garr-sum, you and me. Perhaps we will find a worthy tavern where we can celebrate our pending adventure."

Telrin-vak let out a muted sigh and answered, "As you say, Seventh." He reached out to open the portal and stepped out of the cabin wanting nothing more than to return to the control cabin. He had his orders.

CHAPTER 6

Shad-var Swift-Raider Dominator
GC 43921-CYAN-7-3, Garr-sum Waystation
1582:200:12:16:00 KT (2215AUG08 05:38 CUT)

The trip to Garr-sum was an uneventful thirty-three rotations, during which Leeyak-dar had ample time to wonder just what type of trophy his Voice found for him. The location of storehouses filled with advanced technology seemed too perfect to hope for, so he quickly discarded that notion. More reasonable would be the coordinates of some underdefended colony that *Dominator* could raid with impunity, culling a hold-full of slaves in repeated visits. That would certainly fill the band's coffers with a steady stream of profit, and any technology they might plunder from said colony would serve as a bonus. To Dar's mind, this would be the ideal opportunity and so he focused on it during his waking moments throughout the long journey, dissecting the possibilities and formulating solutions to the various potential setbacks his mind envisioned.

The actual arrival in the Hosh-lek system proved something of a letdown. Since the band had no staff or holdings in the system, they received only the most perfunctory greeting from the world's orbital controller. Despite Shad-var's membership in the Eighteen, they were relegated to an anchorage at the outer shell of the space station's zone, well away from the ships belonging to the five bands that dominated the planet below.

Eventually, a brief message reached *Dominator*, advising the Seventh of the time and place for the planned meeting. After scanning the text, he looked to Telrin-vak to inform him, "I expected to meet on the waystation, but it seems our host wishes to gather on the world below."

The ship's master considered that for only a moment before answering, "I do not trust this plan. We have no people on Garr-sum; this could be a trap."

Leeyak-dar tossed his head to the side. "We have no people on the station either, so the possibility of a danger is equal. But what would be the point of drawing us all the way here? Any intrigue was just as likely to happen at Mid-port. Why here?"

Telrin-vak took more time to consider the possibilities. "Perhaps it comes from one of the Eighteen that are strong here? Just as we would feel safer within our districts on Trogok," he offered.

The Seventh snapped his jaw. "No. Not one of the Eighteen; not even Keev-nur. And never within their own district – it would be too simple for our people to trace," he explained, then thought further on the idea. "If they were to act, it would be through a band with no known ties. Someone who would lead us on a wild hunt in the wrong direction." He let the data-plate drop to his side. "In either case, it is irrelevant."

Vak was startled. "You plan to go along with this? Knowing it is a trap?"

"I plan to go along, suspecting this may be a trap," Leeyak-dar corrected. Seeing the look in the master's eyes, he added, "There is no need for concern. I plan to take our raid-master in the event that our unnamed host has any plans that might alarm you."

The master bent his neck in acceptance. "I will accompany you."

"You will remain here," Dar corrected, perhaps a bit too quickly. "The lander is small enough; I will not be crammed into it as cargo." *Dominator's* little landing craft was meant to ferry supplies up from a planetary surface, and then only in an emergency. As a swift raider, the ship's primary auxiliary was designed to carry a team of raiders to board other ships – not to launch an attack on some small colony. If that turned out to be the type of target the Seventh's Eyes found for them, they would need to acquire a more suitable landing craft.

"Seventh," Telrin-vak pressed.

A quick snap of Leeyak-dar's jaws stopped the old male. When Dar was First of Shad-var, the old master would never have dared disagree with his superior ... certainly not in the control cabin. But since his demotion, Dar occasionally felt the need to explain his reasoning to ensure his crew that his current course of action would not result in a repeat of the failure that earned that loss of stature. "I need you here, in *Dominator*. As you noted, we are not in a strong position here. I will not have the local leadership think they can interfere with our actions in this place. Especially if I am depriving you of Kalgun-dev's presence."

Telrin-vak sneered. "I do not need the raid-master to keep any intruders from coming into our ship," he assured Leeyak-dar, then bent his neck low. "As always, it will be as you say, Seventh. When do you depart?"

Dar lifted the plate once more. "It is already mid-dark in this world's second city; six *garm-liktee* ahead of real-time," he explained, noting the difference between the planet's local chronometer and the standard clock used aboard all ships of the band. "I will travel at first-light next-mark. If the meeting goes as I expect, I will be back in *Dominator* before new-dark on Garr-sum."

District 4
Second City, Garr-sum, Hosh-lek (Kepler-448)
1582:201:05:17:00 KT (2215AUG08 05:38 CUT)

The little lander settled on the hard surface, kicking up a spray of dust that slowly settled around the small craft. Leeyak-dar looked out of the forward window and shuddered slightly at the sight. Garr-sum was a world with a breathable atmosphere, but unlike Trogok it was far from ideal for Krayd-kind. Large sections of the world were little more than desert and even the areas around the second largest city were dry for long stretches of the planet's shorter-than-average orbit. And this-mark was in the middle of those periods. Add to that the planet received less warmth from its small sun than their home world did, so the outside temperatures tended to always be cooler than his species preferred. The only advantage to Garr-sum was that gravity on this world was less than on Krayd-da, so he should find moving around the city less tiring than he did when he visited Trogok, where everything seemed to be a ninth heavier.

Dar pulled the thick cloak tight around himself, making sure to secure the hood that covered his twin crests. From the notes he read on his data-plate, this was the preferred way for visitors to protect their dorsal nostrils from the ever-present dust during the city's dry season. He moved to the hatch as Kalgun-dev extricated himself from the steerer station. The big male duplicated the Seventh's actions, pulling his own cloak around him and securing the hood, though the plain cloth wrap appeared to be much smaller given his frame. With a duck of his head, he signaled he was ready.

A chill wind struck Leeyak-dar's exposed hands as the hatch opened and he stepped down quickly, moving with purpose towards the shelter of the landing field's arrival hall and leaving the raid-master to reseal the hatch on their small craft. Fortunately, *Dominator's* lander was much smaller than others that were now scattered around the landing field and this allowed them to maneuver to a spot closer to the line of structures that bounded the flat plane. Once inside the outer portal, it took only a few moments for the overhead air jets to blast away any dust that had a chance to settle on the two travelers as they crossed the short distance from their vehicle.

When the inner portal finally opened, Leeyak-dar was startled by a familiar voice as he entered the main hall. "Seventh," Shurvil-maj exclaimed as she moved forward to stand before him. "I have secured a conveyance."

"What are you doing here?" Leeyak-dar demanded as he grabbed the female by the arm and hustled her away to a far corner of the greeting chamber; he had no desire to have this encounter witnessed by the gaggle of travelers moving about the space. To his credit, Kalgun-dev followed at a discreet distance to avoid the possibility of the Seventh's wrath spilling over unto him.

Oddly, Shurvil-maj displayed confusion at Dar's reaction to her greeting. "I am completing the arrangements for your meeting, Seventh," she sputtered while staring at the grip Dar had around her arm. "That is my task, is it not?"

"You should be on Kray-da!" Leeyak-dar hissed through gritted teeth. "You are my Voice; you speak for me when I am unavailable. You are meant to watch our holdings."

"Be at calm, Seventh," Shurvil-maj answered in soothing tones. "Arrangements are made; the staff has clear instructions that should suffice to keep all in balance until my return." Despite the Seventh's obvious anger, Maj displayed no fear or panic. "It is my belief that I best serve you in securing the information you require."

Leeyak-dar was far from assured. "And what of Rolehn-dru? What will our Ninth be doing while we are both absent from Ryok-dura?"

"He will do nothing of consequence," Maj replied, maintaining her calm. "The attender I assigned to him will see to that. She has proven quite adept at managing his thoughts and words in the nine-marks since your departure. There is no reason to believe that will change."

Dar could not decide which thought appalled him more. The idea that the dolt he had elevated to Ninth was so stupid as to be led around by the snout by the female intended to assist him, or the possibility that this practice was commonplace among the attenders working for the numerous principals and commanders of the bands. Had Leeyak-dar been so managed in the past? *Am I being subtlety influenced at this very moment?* In truth, he wasn't certain.

The Seventh saw no point in arguing the female's reasoning, and instead turned to the logistics. "How did you get here? No band ships have reason to travel to Garr-sum, so which of our competitors knows you are here?"

"None," Maj answered confidently. "I arranged for a sale to a minor band here and traveled within *Abundance* as it made the delivery from Trogok," she explained, citing one of Shad-var's small cargo haulers. "You may hear some complaint from the Keev-nur; I was forced to undercut their margins by a considerable amount. But none noticed my presence within the ship, nor did any observe my absence before *Abundance* returned to Kray-da."

Dar had to admit surprise – he would have bet the old cargo ship would not be able to make the journey to Garr-sum without sending out a call for rescue. But he could safely ignore any objections from

Keev-nur; though they were one of the Eighteen with assets here, that fact gave them no special rights to the system. Indeed, they were more likely to note the presence of *Dominator* in orbit than a simple delivery by *Abundance*. Despite the unusual circumstances, it appeared his Voice successfully navigated the obstacles before her. He snapped his jaw before ordering, "Take us to this conveyance. I wish to conclude our business here before anyone has time to notice *Dominator* circling this world."

The groundrunner was a non-descript vehicle quickly lost in a sea of nearly-identical peers. The driver remained silent as she followed a circuitous path to their destination. Even though he wasn't a resident of the city, Leeyak-dar recognized that the route was intended to expose and deter anyone who might be following them. Such action would likely prove fruitless in Ryok-dura or any other city on Kray-da, but here the near constant layer of dust that floated through the streets served to obscure the distinguishing features of their groundrunner at a distance of more than a handful of *zel-kray*.

Shurvil-maj was pleased the Seventh did not further question her decision to travel to this distant world. She could hardly tell him the truth – that she suspected the intelligence she provided to him over the past nine-marks. Far too many of the easy targets she gave him proved to be anything but easy; too many were better protected than they were told, or carried less valuable cargo than was promised. Maj could not afford to have her sponsor lose faith in her abilities. Not that Maj's belief in herself ever wavered; she was confident in her skills. Instead, she questioned her sources. Many targets were provided by members of Shad-var or their allies that Maj never worked with before, and the results were disappointing. The Voice of the Seventh wanted to meet this latest contact face-to-face to better evaluate his sincerity.

When they finally arrived at their destination, the driver pulled into a *porte-cochère*-like extension that briefly sealed at both ends before blasting the vehicle with air to scrub away the accumulated dust. Once the operators thought the groundrunner was sufficiently clean, the doors opened, and Kalgun-dev moved to alight.

"Remain nearby. I will call when we are ready to return," Shurvil-maj informed the driver before she preceded Leeyak-dar out of the vehicle.

There was no attender stationed in the foyer of the building, just a simple directory with colored blocks next to office numbers. Maj pulled a small device from inside her cloak and led the trio to an ascender. They emerged several levels above the streets outside to an empty passageway. Another glance at her guide, and Maj led them to a portal with a small magenta and brown block positioned to the side. The Voice of the Seventh pressed her device to the block and the portal rolled away, granting them access.

As with the foyer, the antechamber was empty, missing the attender most any office by rights should have. By reflex, Leeyak-dar's tongue flicked out to taste the air, hoping to gain some clue to the peculiarity. As he looked around the spare room, Shurvil-maj unfastened and removed her cloak. Beneath she was wearing her usual teal-blue leathers, though missing were any marks that might identify her position or even membership in the Shad-var band. Leeyak-dar and Kalgun-dev were similarly unmarked, but that was common practice when working on any raider. *What is Maj's reason for such action?* "Where is your badge, Voice?" the Seventh inquired.

Shurvil-maj glanced down to the spot on her vest where her badge of office normally rested and answered, "In Ryok-dura. I thought it best to not draw attention to my travels, and so wore a simple work suit while traveling in *Abundance*." She extended her arms outward, adding, "I thought this would be more appropriate for our current task."

Leeyak-dar shook his head in approval as he shrugged out of his own cloak. "A wise precaution. I should expect no less."

Any further discussion was interrupted by the sound of the next portal opening. A male stepped out and Leeyak-dar quickly sized him up. The male was younger and of moderate stature and build, wearing a leather tunic with sleeves that extended beyond his elbows and britches that nearly reached his ankles; the suit no doubt an accommodation to the chill temperatures of this world. The chartreuse leathers contrasted sharply against the male's muddy green scales and his left crest was adorned by a single strip of polished nickel. Despite his humble appearance, the Krayd exuded confidence to the visitors. "Shurvil-maj, be welcome in the place of Uhl-reej," he exclaimed towards the Seventh's Voice before turning his eye towards Dar. "This must be your commander. Welcome greater sir." The yet unidentified male ducked his head to the right in an overly dramatic sign of subservience.

"I must be," Leeyak-dar agreed coldly, offering the stranger as little information as possible. Uhl-reej was a minor band, based entirely on Garr-sum and allied with none of the Eighteen as far as Dar could recall. That explained why he did not recognize the magenta and brown colors that marked the outer portal. He gestured to the empty space asking, "Do we discuss our business out here?"

The ingratiating look on the male's face never wavered. "If that is your desire, Commander. I thought we would be more comfortable in my office," he answered, bending slightly as he waved his guests into the following chamber.

The next room was only slightly better furnished than the last, with a small table surrounded by six benches in the center of the room. To one side, a narrow shelf was adorned with an assortment of bowls containing a selection of meats and what Dar's nose assumed was fermented fruit juices. "Please, partake in the bounty of Uhl-reej," their host offered as he followed Shurvil-maj into the room and closed the portal behind him.

Despite a third of an orbit subsisting on the rations available on the band's lowly swift raider, Leeyak-dar ignored the offering, choosing instead to stand near the main table. "Perhaps. Once our business is concluded," he answered for the group. Kalgun-dev and Shurvil-maj knew better than to dissent from that decision.

"As you wish," their host replied, then moved to the table, waiting for Leeyak-dar to select his bench before sitting himself on the opposite side. The Voice and raid-master took up their positions on either side of the Seventh. Leaning forward to lower his head, the male announced, "I am Hymrek-po, Ear to the Third of Uhl-reej."

Dar let this revelation hang in the air for several breaths before returning, "I am Leeyak-dar, Seventh of Shad-var."

Po's upper lip pulled back in the hint of a sneer. "I suspected as much when I finally saw you. You are notable among the senior members of the Eighteen, known even here on far off Garr-sum." He dipped his head again. "Welcome, mighty Seventh."

The fawning did nothing to improve Leeyak-dar's opinion of Hymrek-po. "You have something you wish to trade. What is it?" he demanded.

Recognizing that his usual charms would not work on this individual, Hymrek-po leaned back on his bench and moved into his sales pitch. "As I said, I am Ear to the Third, collecting information that may be of use to our band. Sometimes ... sometimes the information I acquire cannot be used by us. When this happens, I seek others who may wish to purchase what I know."

Leeyak-dar did not travel thirty rotations to be played with by some minor functionary of a backwater band. "And what do you have to sell, shop minder?" he growled, reducing the Uhl-reej lieutenant to the ranks of simple laborer.

Hymrek-po ignored the intended slight. Instead, he reached into his tunic and extracted a small data-leaf, the coppery finish of its surface glinting in the overhead lighting. "I have the location of ships. Ships ready ... no, waiting to be collected by a worthy crew of raiders," he teased.

Finally satisfied that they were progressing, Leeyak-dar held out a hand as Shurvil-maj slid a data-plate towards her commander. Hymrek-po pulled back slightly, producing a similar if older device from beneath the table with his other hand. He slid the data-leaf into the Uhl-reej device before offering it to Dar. "My reader if you don't mind. I'm sure you understand," he offered as explanation.

The Seventh of Shad-var accepted the plate, then flicked through the contents on the screen. Several panels of text were followed by a collection of blurry images of hulls hanging in the dark of space; no world was nearby. Despite their poor quality, one or two of the images looked familiar to Leeyak-dar. The text referred to several eighteens of ships, though the images accounted for only six. "Impressive," he murmured as he reached the end of the data on the leaf, then looked up. "What is to prevent me from simply walking out with this?"

Hymrek-po leaned back before explaining, "If you were to do that, a blast of energy would fill the offices the moment you crossed through that portal. The blast is designed to wipe all data from the leaf and plate." He turned his attention to Shurvil-maj as she toyed with the Shad-var data-plate she originally offered to her Seventh. "As well as any devices you may be carrying if you planned to make copies," he warned. Returning his attention to Dar, he finished, "I am told the energy will also make all of us very sick for a nine-mark, at least. So, I ask that you refrain from a pointless attempt to cheat me."

Dar's upper lip peeled back in the equivalent of a grin. *Finally, some evidence that I am not dealing with a simple underling*, he thought. He placed the data-plate on the table. "You take precautions. Do many of those who buy from you decide it is easier to take what they want?"

"I do not treat you as a fool, great Seventh of Shad-var. There is no need to treat me as one," Hymrek-po returned flatly. "I deal in information, not physical goods. My wares require special protection from those who think Uhl-reej too weak to defend our property."

Leeyak-dar flicked the Ear's data-plate forward. "And, of course, you provide only a sample. Not enough for us to act; only what is needed to get my attention. Such as leaving out the fact that those ships are of *hooman* design."

Hymrek-po reached forward and retrieved his device, placing it under his hands on the table. "No need to mention that to you, Seventh. As you just proved."

Leeyak-dar's heart quickened; this exchange was proving better than he had hoped. Casually he pointed out, "*Hooman* space is far beyond Mid-port. I was not aware the Uhl-reej roamed so far from the familiar stars. Just how did you come by this knowledge?"

Hymrek-po shrugged. "While we may not journey as far as the Eighteen, our ships frequently pass beyond Mid-port. And when you are truly patient, the quarry will come to you," he offered. "In this case, a *hooman* hauler was found powerless by one of our raiders. It offered no resistance and yielded several captives. Most were of the blue-skinned variety, but one had the sickly pink coloration. It was also the most pathetic, squealing and bleating for release. It offered all this and more for its survival," he explained while tapping the data-plate.

Dar's head wobbled in thought. "And you can provide this *hooman* as part of any agreement," he interjected.

"Sadly, no," Hymrek-po replied. "Our Third was eager to sell the slaves; mammals are well suited to this world and fetch a high price. It is ... no longer available."

"You cannot reveal the buyer," Leeyak-dar translated. "Then what am I buying, if you have already sold the source of this information to another?"

Hymrek-po tilted his head to one side. "I offer the complete information, including the *hooman's* personal data device. It is the source of the images you witnessed but contains much more which we have been unable to extract." He toyed with data-plate under his hand. "No doubt Shad-var has more experience in this area and will make quick work of it."

"No doubt," Leeyak-dar agreed, but pressed his objection. "Still, someone holds the slave, and it could reveal much of this from memory." His eyes drifted over the Uhl-reej's crests. "And I don't think you will reveal who has this slave now so that we can retrieve it and eliminate any risk of the information leaking out."

Hymrek-po placed his hands palm-upward on the table. "You understand, I cannot give that information any more than I can tell others of your purchase. To do that would harm my band's reputation." He brought his hands together as he leaned closer, confiding, "But you can be certain that the *hooman* will not further share any information it holds. Before it was sold, we removed its tongue to silence its noises. Such method is very effective with mammals, and it was the only way we could make it suitable for the buyers. No one wants a noisy slave."

Leeyak-dar silently considered those words. To his mind, Uhl-reej had no reputation to protect, but it was common practice to keep any transactions private between the two bands, so he excepted the confidence. As for the removal of the slave's tongue, such action was of little use when dealing with Ooverg or other Krayd-like aliens, but Dar knew his own band's slave masters made use of the practice with the blue-skin *hoomans* in their pens. So long as it was done before delivery, whatever secrets this pink-skin held should be unobtainable by its current owners. "That should be enough," he murmured, but then turned to the final question. "If all this is true, what prevents Uhl-reej from acting on this information you have so dutifully protected?"

Hymrek-po remained silent for a stretch, as if to build up anticipation at the reveal of some hidden agenda. "Our First is a cautious male, seeking the slow but steady path to enrichment. In that, I hear he has much in common with your own band's current principal." He glanced to the food on the shelf, his tongue flicking slowly. It was clear he wished to partake of one of the bowls but would not allow any interruption to derail the negotiations. "And my Third chooses not to oppose him in this instance. As you yourself said, our three raiders have never traveled as far as this space, and he had no wish to take the chance now. No, these prizes require a band with far more resources than we can bring forward." He shrugged once more. "Of course, if you are not interested, there are other bands who can easily match the power of the Shad-var."

Leeyak-dar sneered at the veiled insult since it was such an obvious play to the Shad-var commander's vanity. And he very much doubted Uhl-reej could field as many ships as their male just claimed, paltry number though it was. No; he had seen and heard enough and decided it was time to bring the negotiations to a close. "What do you seek for all of this?" he asked coldly.

The Ear of the Third swayed on his bench, explaining, "I have no doubt that partnership between Shad-var and Uhl-reej would be of benefit to both ..."

"A number," the Seventh demanded. He had no desire to drag this on any further and refused to be the first to place a price on what he was buying, a sign of weakness whenever haggling. And he certainly wasn't going to wait for some overarching agreement between their bands.

Hymrek-po leaned back slightly at the rebuff while maintaining an easy air. "I believe one-ninth share in the first prize, plus eight-ninths of a ninth share in the following eight prizes would be agreeable," he offered.

Dar sneered. "Eight-ninths of a ninth share in the first prize, then six-ninths of a ninth in the following five prizes," he returned with a harsh look.

Hymrek-po raised his hands upward, suggesting, "I am certain there are others of the Eighteen who would agree with our modest requirements."

"Then call them," Leeyak-dar challenged and pressed his hands down on the table as he rose from his bench. Glancing to the two silent members of his band, he announced, "We are done."

The Uhl-reej panicked. "Please. You misunderstand. I was merely offering an opinion," he rambled desperately. "I am sure that my Third will agree to your assessment. We are not merely interested in a single deal; we seek to work with you on future exchanges here on Garr-sum." He leaned forward to stage whisper, "Uhl-reej can act as your agents on this world."

Leeyak-dar counted slowly to nine before returning to his bench. "Such an arrangement might be possible. It will depend of course on the outcome of this first endeavor," he offered. If soothing words about possible future events were enough to secure the information he needed, Dar had no qualms about making those noises. His only concern was locating this promised prize.

"Then we have an agreement," Hymrek-po declared, eager to seal the deal before Dar had a chance to squeeze him further on the price. "I will prepare the contract for your approval."

Leeyak-dar was careful to give away any sign of pleasure in his reply. "We have an agreement," he blandly concurred.

CHAPTER 7

Shad-var Swift-Raider Dominator
GC 43921-CYAN-7-3, Garr-sum Waystation
1582:201:11:03:03 KT (2215AUG08 12:36 CUT)

The trip back to *Dominator* was made largely in silence; Leeyak-dar and Kalgun-dev took their previous seats in the lander while Shurvil-maj was forced to endure the spare bench in the back next to her travel chest and the items they purchased on the planet. The Voice's brief time on Garr-sum quickly came to an end.

Once the little lander was safely within Dominator's hold, Telrin-vak greeted them at the portal and the Seventh lost no time organizing their next steps. "Master, clear the feeding cabin. We must discuss our next venture," Dar ordered as he stepped through the opening.

"Already done, Seventh," Vak returned, then looked to their newest passenger. "You are lucky, Voice. Since we are under-crewed, an empty cabin is available for you on the lower level."

"That won't be needed; she does not travel with us," Leeyak-dar declared as he strode down the long connectway to *Dominator's* forward main module. "Keep her chest in the hold; Shurvil-maj will leave us once our planning is done."

No one questioned this decision and the four continued on in silence, finally reaching their destination. As a swift raider, Dominator lacked the normal planning cabin found on larger ships. Instead, the Seventh commandeered the largest cabin on the ship to serve this function. The feeding cabin was dominated by a single large table in the center of the room with six benches waiting on either side. While there were no discarded bowls visible on the table or the shelves that ringed the cabin, the smell of food still hung in the air. Leeyak-dar's tongue flicked out by reflex in response to the odor and he stopped dead in his tracks the moment he set foot in the cabin.

"Bring bowls of water," he ordered Shurvil-maj; he would feed once their plans were in place and had no desire to see fermented juices lead to any poor decisions at this stage. He moved to the table and activated the data-plate he brought back from the world below, inserting one of the data-leaves given to them by Hymrek-po while handing the *hooman* data device to Telrin-vak. "Give this to one of your monitors but warn them: any loss of information will be taken from their hides! We must know if this is a match for what we collected from that *hooman* hauler four orbits back," he insisted, referring to a prize the band captured when Dar first planned to reap the bounty of the *hooman* worlds.

The master bent his neck and hurried from the cabin while the Seventh brushed a claw against the surface of his data-plate, connecting the device to the large screen bolted to the wall above the empty shelf. Normally this screen would be used to provide entertainments to the crew as they fed, but now Leeyak-dar planned to make use of it as he mapped out their conquest. The screen flashed to life to reveal an image of space with several blurry streaks of near white marring the otherwise black vista. Each time Dar touched the plate a new picture appeared, until he finally settled on a somewhat better focused image of a light grey hull.

Shurvil-maj came around the table with bowls of water and the trio waited for the ship's master to return. When he did, Leeyak-dar announced, "This is our target!"

Telrin-vak moved closer to settle into his place at the table as he inspected the image. "It looks familiar," he commented.

"It should. You fought these before," the Seventh offered, waiting for the master to finally recognize their prey. When he said nothing, Leeyak-dar chided. "Do you not recall? The raid on the *hooman* world. Where Orval-brak failed to return with our treasure."

A low whistle sounded from Vak's crest as his head bobbed twice. "Yes. They were not strong fighters, but they were agile," he recalled. The image was joined by a block of text giving a few vital statistics on the alien ship. "About the size of a sharp raider, but no match for one. It could prove a challenge for *Dominator*, though," he commented, thinking back to the skirmish he fought against ships like this one four orbits ago. There were larger ships than this one; ships that fought *Silver Bounty* shot for shot. That skirmish marked the beginning of the fall that brought Dar and Vak to their current state.

Leeyak-dar's lips curled. "Not this one. It is uncrewed, with no one to target us as we approach."

Telrin-vak was reaching for the bowl of water and it slipped from his grasp at those words. "How can you be certain?"

Leeyak-dar skipped back through the images to reveal the sea of blurry hulls. "It is one of eighteens of ships the *hoomans* have abandoned in a minor system. All primed and ready for the taking."

The master looked to the others at the table; both Shurvil-maj and Kalgun-dev appeared to accept these words as fact. Still, Vak had his doubts. "That is ridiculous. Why would the *hoomans* save empty hulls? If they still function, they should be in use. If they cannot function, they should be broken down to keep other ships in working order. To just leave them floating about ... it makes no sense," Telrin-vak insisted. "Why would they do this?"

Leeyak-dar dipped his snout in the water to soothe his throat. "Who knows. They are aliens; they don't think the way we do. Perhaps this makes some sense to their mammalian brains," the Seventh offered as explanation.

The old master was not convinced. "Perhaps it is an illusion. Or a trap," he warned. "A deceit that draws in their enemies so they can pounce on the ill-informed."

"You give them too much credit," the Seventh countered, but did not totally dismiss the old male's concerns. "But we will step gently into this space, just in case you are correct."

Telrin-vak was mollified by this concession and his eyes slid down to the plate in front of him when it buzzed. "Our luck holds, Seventh. The location you provided appears on the maps we captured orbits ago," he informed the group and with a sweep of his hand shared the coordinates with Dar's device.

The image and data on the large screen were replaced with a map of Krayd space, green highlights marking the location of Kray-da and the other worlds and ports the various bands now occupied. In a far corner, a purple square flashed around an insignificant star and a thin line offered the shortest route between that location and *Dominator's* current spot above Garr-sum.

It was much further than Leeyak-dar originally imagined and a part of him deflated at that realization.

"More than ninety rotations travel, even at our top speed. And we would be lucky to maintain top speed for that long," Telrin-vak commented as he studied the numbers on his data-plate. He looked up to see the stunned looks on the three others. "It will take much longer if we need to travel to Mid-port for supplies."

"Can this raider travel that far and back?" Shurvil-maj wondered aloud. "Will the supplies last that long?"

"Yes. It can be done," Leeyak-dar said as if trying to convince himself. His voice grew stronger when he realized he had just shown weakness in front of his crew. "Yes," he repeated stronger, his eyes fixed on the long purple line on the screen. "It can be done. Once we take the ship, the prize-crew will be out of *Dominator*. We will need less rations to feed the reduced crew."

"And what of the prize-crew? What will they feed on?" Telrin-vak asked, pointing out the flaw in the Seventh's formula.

Leeyak-dar flicked his tongue out casually. "You recall the *hooman* hauler we captured, Master. It carried food that was … edible. At least some of it. It won't be a feast, but the prize crew will not starve. The air and water will be plenty," he reassured the old male.

"The hauler was not abandoned," Telrin-vak reminded Dar. "Why would any of these ships still carry food if there is no crew to be fed?"

Leeyak-dar finally looked away from the screen to stare at his old shipmate. "Their machines produce their food, Telrin-vak. You know that! All we require is power to feed the prize crew, and that we can guarantee," he assured the trio around him.

Telrin-vak would not bend. "And if those machines are missing or disabled? What then?"

The Seventh was growing weary of the master's pessimism and it no doubt showed on his face as the two others at the table looked to each other.

"We can always forage from any suitable worlds we find along the way, once we are far from *hooman* space," Kalgun-dev offered in a gravelly voice. "And a return to Mid-port will be shorter, so we do not need to double the provisions used for the first part of the journey."

"True," Telrin-vak agreed, for even he finally noticed the stare from his superior. "It will not be easy, but it can be done."

Pleased that his senior crew were finally embracing the plan, Leeyak-dar shifted his gaze to the raid-master. "How many will you need to take the ship?" he asked. He touched a control, and a rough outline of the target replaced the previous image on the screen.

Kalgun-dev stood and moved to stand within arm's length of the image. Studying the representation, he commented, "I will need better plans than these to start." He continued to inspect the information on the screen for several breaths before adding, "As long as the *hoomans* left no traps behind and the ship is truly abandoned, we have enough raiders in *Dominator* to take and hold this ship. Add a steerer and drive crew that can work the alien controls, and it will be enough to slip the ship away from their snouts." He looked to Telrin-vak. "Too many for the lander, and it will take at least two trips in our skiff," he commented before turning back to the screen. "If we really mean to sneak under their eyes, I prefer to have a dark-skiff."

Telrin-vak looked to the Seventh, explaining, "We would need to return to Near-port for one of those. Shad-var has no supplies here."

Leeyak-dar snapped his jaw. "No. That would add nine-marks to the trip. Time we cannot afford."

"Time may not be needed," Shurvil-maj offered. All eyes turned to her as she explained. "I know of a dark-skiff that is available. At the waystation. It is old and you will need to tell me if it meets your needs."

Leeyak-dar stared at the female. "Explain, Voice. You just happen to have the very thing our raid-master seeks? How is that possible?"

If anything, Shurvil-maj looked hurt by the question. "I strive to support you, Seventh. It is my job to anticipate your needs; to see that you are supplied quickly and allow you to focus on more important matters." She looked to the other two males in the cabin. "Since I arrived before you and I am already familiar with all the supplies *Dominator* currently holds, I made use of that time to locate local items that might be needed for your raid."

"And one of those items you located was a dark-skiff?" Telrin-vak asked with a fair amount of skepticism in his voices.

"Yes," the Voice answered simply. She looked to Kalgun-dev and asked, "Are there other supplies you will need? The Vor-thal have four canisters of energy-draining ribbon they wish to sell, though the price they ask would be greater than that of the skiff."

Leeyak-dar's tongue flicked out quickly. "Perhaps we should review what you have found," he suggested, wondering just how he had ever risen to First without this female.

A *garm-liktee* later, the three males hammered out a reasonable course of action, while Shurvil-maj now had a list of items they required. Most of the items were available from the waystation that floated nearby, though one or two items required a return to the surface. Leeyak-dar was still weighing the value of those particular items against the risk of having his agent spotted in one or more of the cities of Garr-sum. Until *Dominator* departed, it was still possible for one of Shad-var's competitors to reach their prize ahead of the swift raider and render all of his plans meaningless.

Once the master and raid-master left the cabin, Leeyak-dar broached the subject. "You will make every attempt to secure these items without leaving the waystation. If that cannot be done, we will depart without them."

Shurvil-maj was taken aback by this order. "Are you certain, Seventh? The Gorrethi blasters ..."

"The Gorrethi blasters would be useful to repel any attempt to retake the ship," Dar readily agreed. These weapons were in short supply and highly sought after by most of the bands; they were more powerful than the standard-issue Krayd models and had the added benefit of rarely causing damage to hulls or other internal components since they could be tuned to limit their destructive energies to animal flesh. The idea that there were four to be had in the first city was tempting, but not tempting enough. "But that is unlikely to happen; the ship will be gone before the *hoomans* can react. And I will not risk the Rek-thued learning of our need and seeking a share in the treasure," he explained. It was enough that the Uhl-reej were included; he would not have another partner. That path led to trouble as he well knew from experience. *Never again.*

Shurvil-maj bent her neck. "It will be as you say, Seventh. I will go to the waystation and secure what is available there. Then I return with the dark-skiff," she agreed.

"No. As I already said, you will not travel with us in *Dominator*," the Seventh reminded her. "There is a Bar-chuk cargo hauler traveling to Kray-da in five rotations. Our band exchanges with them frequently and they will not refuse to carry one of our overseers back to the home world."

Shurvil-maj was disappointed by this decision. "I should be with you, Seventh. I have shown my usefulness for this raid."

"You will do as I say, Voice!" Leeyak-dar returned a little louder than was needed in the empty cabin, the tones from his crest echoing off the barren walls, the claws of his hands spreading out as if to strike the wayward female. "You will return to Ryok-dura and see that our operations remain profitable. And you will await my return with the prize!" With the words spat out, his hands relaxed, and his tone softened. "Once we capture this first ship, I will remain on Kray-da for a time and you can travel with the raiders to retrieve more *hooman* treasure." He offered this last in an attempt to mollify any anger Maj might have at being excluded from such a profitable endeavor. He could ill afford to lose such a valuable asset in his quest to return to higher position.

To his relief, Shurvil-maj bobbed her head gently and whistled agreement. "I will perform as instructed, Seventh. You have no need to concern yourself with trivial matters in Ryok-dura; all will be as you left it ... with a healthy increase in silver that will more than cover any expenses incurred at the waystation," she informed him. "I will also make arrangements at Mid-port for your return there."

Leeyak-dar looked past Shurvil-maj at the screen on the far wall, a blank slate that only moments before was used to outline his return to glory. For a breath, he imagined the sight of returning to Mid-port with his newest prize-ship. "Good," he grunted, more to himself than to his underling.

Shad-var Tower, District 38
Ryok-dura, Oover-telz, Kray-da, Hosh
1582:205:10:05:10 KT (2215AUG12 11:17 CUT)

Orval-geeth was pacing in her office when the harsh buzz sounded from her desk, and she hurried across the moss floor to reach her device. Grabbing the data-plate, she stabbed at the flashing symbol and skimmed the text that popped up. After taking in the key points, she reread the missive more thoroughly to be certain there was no crucial item she missed in her hurried first pass. As a result, she did not notice the portal to her office open until a voice interrupted her thoughts.

"Eyes, has any news of our missing Seventh arrived," Sselmin-dor inquired. When he noticed her attention to the screen before he asked, "Is that it?"

Geeth looked up while surreptitiously clearing and deleting the message she just received. "No, First. Nothing since the original report that *Dominator* was in the Hosh-lek system," she informed her superior.

The First of Shad-var snapped his jaws. "This is not acceptable. It is two seasons since he was given that raider, and we have seen little treasure in return. Now he squanders time at Garr-sum where we have no business and any supplies his ship needs will probably cost us double!" The claws on his right hand were flexing during this rant. "The favor of the Chief can only excuse so much!"

"I will contact the Ninth to see if there is any explanation for this behavior," Orval-geeth offered.

After the uncustomary display of anger, Dor replied in calmer voices, "No. There is no point; our Ninth will know nothing. Rolehn-dru is duller than a stone, and not nearly as useful. The only reason Leeyak-dar elevated him was because he could be counted on to do nothing that would disrupt Dar's plans." He snorted. "The Voice of the Seventh will know the true reason for this action."

"I am told she is on Trogok, First," Orval-geeth cooed before deciding to nudge her principal with the thought, "Though I can find no trace of her there in several rotations."

Sselmin-dor stared at his Eyes for a moment. "You think she is elsewhere? Where? Do you suggest Garr-sum?"

Orval-geeth shrugged. "I cannot speculate; I can only report what I have learned."

The First considered this aloud, "Certainly not Garr-sum. What business does she have there? But then, what reason does *Dominator* have to be there?" He walked to the chamber's window, staring out at the rooftops that led as steps down to the water. After several breaths, he finally turned back. "You are my Eyes; learn what is happening and why! I will not have this. I must know what is going on beneath my snout."

"It will be as you say, First," Orval-geeth replied to the male's back as he exited her office. Satisfied with the brief exchange, she settled onto her bench and returned to her data-plate.

JOHN LALLIER

CHAPTER 8

Uhl-reej Building, District 6
Second City, Garr-sum, Hosh-lek (Kepler-448)
1582:208:11:07:08 KT (2215AUG15 12:38 CUT)

Hymrek-po hurried up the incline to the top level of the building and continued down the corridor, skidding to a stop just in front of his destination. He glanced down, tugging at the edges of his tunic in an effort to hide any sign of exertion that might have resulted from his unanticipated journey to the domain of the band's elite. The summons he received left no doubt as to the urgency.

At his touch, the portal rolled open and the Ear of the Third stepped into the antechamber. The normally perky attender seated at the desk recognized Hymrek-po immediately and triggered the next portal to open even as he strode forward. Normally he would engage the young female in idle chatter as he waited for his moment with the office's owner, but this-mark was different. This-mark he was ushered straight in.

"How could you do this?" his master bellowed when Hymrek-po stepped into the main office. The Third of Uhl-reej was a young male, barely an orbit or two older than Po, though there the similarities ended. While Hymrek-po would never be considered a fierce male like most of the band's raiders, he was at least in reasonable shape for a male of thirty-five orbits. Zhaymog-ssel, on the other claw, was a rotund little male who looked at least nine (and more likely eighteen) orbits older as the *triknar* leather stretched and cracked as it tried to cover his bulging belly. The pair of lenses that dangled before his eyes in an attempt to compensate for his failing vision did nothing to enhance his appearance. Where the First of the band was an elder schemer and the Second was a seasoned raider, the Third of Uhl-reej was little more than a bead-counter, with the appearance that went with that stereotype. Indeed, the only thing about Ssel that exhibited any strength was his voices as the Third yelled at his lieutenant, "How did you let this happen? Explain this!"

Po stopped a full *zel-kray* in front of the Third's desk as he ducked his head to the side. "I will of course try to answer your questions as well as I am able, Third," he offered humbly. "If you would just tell me what matter has caused you such concern."

Zhaymog-ssel slapped the desk in front of him as his jaws snapped repeatedly. "This!" he screamed, and he picked up a data-plate and flung it at Po. Fortunately for the Ear of the Third, his master's lack of physical prowess resulted in the device clattering to the floor at Hymrek-po's feet, well short of causing any harm to its intended target. For his part, the Third took no notice of his failure as he growled, "I've been on the caller with the Fourth of Gil-mot for nearly a *garm-liktee*. Do you know how much business we do with the Gil-mot?" It was clear that in his current state, Ssel was not going to wait for an answer. "A third! A full third of our business last orbit was with Gil-mot. And now, their Fourth is threatening to cancel all our agreements!"

Hymrek-po bent to retrieve the data-plate from the thin turf of the floor. Any hope that the device might have been damaged in its truncated flight was dashed as the screen sprang to life at his touch. The Gil-mot were a small band in comparison to the Eighteen, but far larger than Uhl-reej, with holdings both here on Garr-sum as well as on Trogok. Despite the range of transactions Gil-mot had with Uhl-reej, Hymrek-po only rarely had dealings with that particular band. There was only one this orbit that he recalled, and an uneasy feeling filled him. Po's fears were confirmed as he read through the text on the data-plate's screen. "Ah. The slaves," he commented.

"Yes! The slaves! The slaves you sold them. Apparently, without checking them out thoroughly," Zhaymog-ssel loudly confirmed. "One of them died last-mark."

Hymrek-po returned a quizzical look, explaining after a check of the plate, "We sold those slaves nearly three nine-marks ago. They cannot hold us at fault for the loss of a single slave. Everyone knows how quickly the Gil-mot go through slaves ... the way they overwork them. Especially the mammals."

Zhaymog-ssel slapped the desk again. "It didn't die of overwork! I wouldn't call you up here if that was the case!" he sharply reminded his underling. "It died of some disease. Something their slave-master has never seen before. Foaming at the mouth! Screaming!" he recounted with a shudder as he imagined the sight.

"Which one?" Hymrek-po asked as he casually scanned through the remaining text on the device.

"Which one?" Zhaymog-ssel repeated in surprise. "Which one? Who cares which one. The problem is: now they think the whole batch is infected. To make matters worse, they sent half of the slaves we sold them to Trogok. So now they think the band's whole herd is at risk!"

Finally finding the information he was looking for, Po looked up. "It was the pink," he announced as if that revelation was the answer to their problems.

Ssel threw up his hands. "Pink. Blue. Maroon. What does it matter?" he demanded.

Hymrek-po fell back into his sales-male voice. "Everyone knows the pinks are not as sturdy as the blues. They're different breeds. They probably cannot spread diseases to each other. And definitely not to the other mammals in the Gil-mot herd. All this worry is unneeded."

"Probably? Probably cannot spread?" the Third scoffed. "The Fourth of Gil-mot is not going to be satisfied with probably. Why weren't these slaves checked before we sold them?"

Po fought to keep the sneer from his lips. "You insisted that we sell them quickly, Third. You did not wish to wait and go through the marketplace," he reminded his principal. "The slave market has examiners who might have caught any disease unique to the pinks. Our slave-master checked them as best he could, but we don't get *hoomans* that often. Still, there was only the one pink. If this was a disease, it ended with that one death." He saw that the Third still had doubts about his assessment. "I know a band on Trogok that has more experience with this breed. I will contact them to see if they have any knowledge of this particular problem," he offered.

Zhaymog-ssel considered all this for a few breaths before whistling agreement. "Be certain to keep this information confidential, but don't pay too much for it," he instructed. "I will speak again with the Gil-mot Fourth to tell him of our ... expert assessment."

Hymrek-po bent his neck at the order, adding, "It is unfortunate, but we do not have any *hoomans* to offer as compensation for the lost slave. We do have a Balthod we can give them."

The Third snapped his jaws at the suggestion, which caused his lenses to jangle. "There is no need to be too hasty. We cannot even be certain that this dead slave was the result of disease; as you said, it might be a response to the treatment it received from its new owners." As expected, the bead-counter in Zhaymog-ssel could always be counted on to emerge when the topic turned to payments.

"It will be as you say, Third," Po agreed as he moved forward and gently placed the data-plate back on the Third's desk. With the storm now passed, he asked, "Do you require anything else?"

Zhaymog-ssel turned his chair to give him a better view of the screen mounted on the near wall. "No, nothing. Just get me that answer from Trogok," he responded, his attention clearly having moved off to other matters.

Hymrek-po exited the office without a word and waited until he was well down the corridor before he pulled out his own data-plate. A scroll through the incoming messages on an obscure account confirmed his suspicion. A recent deposit to his covert account was made last-mark, within a *garm-liktee* of the Gil-mot slave's death. A final transaction from his mysterious partner.

He continued back down the incline to his own office with mixed emotions. While he was pleased by the unexpected addition to his fortunes, he was also saddened to think this might be his last dealings with his unknown benefactor. *Whoever that Krayd was*, he thought, *he really knows how to run a scheme. I just wonder how it will all turn out.*

A sudden thought made him stumble on the ramp. Was it possible the death of the slave was only the beginning? If the point was to obscure any trail that might lead back to his unknown partner, would Hymrek-po be the next one eliminated? That idea quickly erased any happiness Po found in his recent windfall.

Shad-var Building, District 2
Ryok-dura, Oover-telz, Kray-da, Hosh
1582:218:10:12:14 KT (2215AUG25 11:18 CUT)

Shurvil-maj was in the office by six *garm-liktee* to review all the correspondence that built up during her absence. Traveling on the Bar-chuk cargo hauler prevented her from accessing any secure messages, since these were limited to systems owned and operated by that band. Some might have seen this as an opportunity to relax, but to Maj it was torture. Better to have no access and be sick in her nest than to have only partial access to the mundane, unencrypted messages and have to guess what else she was missing.

After four *garm-liktee*, she was only through five-ninths of the backlog when a buzz from the door announced a visitor. Since none were scheduled, Shurvil-maj had to assume that the summoner was important, or the attender in the antechamber would have dismissed them. As she rose from her bench, the door opened and revealed the newcomer.

"Voice of the Seventh, I hope this does not interrupt you," Orval-geeth offered as she strode into the office. She paused, waiting for the door to close behind her before she followed, "You have been away so long. How was your visit to Trogok?"

Shurvil-maj ducked her head to the right in a show of modesty. Though they were both lieutenants, Orval-geeth's attachment to the First clearly put her above the Voice of the Seventh. "My travels were strictly functional; I spent most of my time in ships and waystations. Unfortunately, I was not able to see Trogok for myself," she answered as a way to deflect the question without resorting to an outright lie. Through her connections, Maj did not doubt that Orval-geeth knew exactly which ship brought the Voice back to Kray-da, as well as the last planet that Bar-chuk hauler visited.

Rather than challenge the falsehood, Orval-geeth looked about, taking inventory of the room. "Still, it is good to have you back, tending to business. You appear quite at home in this place."

"I am Voice of the Seventh. It is right that I am here when he is away, to act in his place while he raids for Shad-var," Shurvil-maj returned indignantly.

Geeth looked down her snout at Maj. "Of course. Our Seventh is fortunate to have you as his Voice. To serve him during his raids. Still, I do not believe any expected him to be away quite so long. I wonder if some may soon forget that he is Seventh by the time he returns."

Shurvil-maj held her neck high, insisting, "It is not unusual for a ship to be out raiding for most of an orbit. Especially when they are chasing prizes!"

"Ah, so Leeyak-dar has prizes in his sights," Orval-geeth pounced. "That is good news. After reading the reports from the Second, I feared that *Dominator* would continue to cost more than it brings in. When can I tell the First to expect one of these prizes?"

Shurvil-maj realized her misstep and quickly retreated. "As I said, ships can be out for nearly an orbit at a time. All I know is that Leeyak-dar will return to Mid-port when *Dominator's* holds are full of treasure and a worthy prize has been secured," she spouted, then attempted to alter the topic. "You know his habits; you once served under him." In her anger, she may have stressed the concept of 'under' more than was wise.

If anything, Orval-geeth was pleased that she could so easily rattle the normally staid composure of Shurvil-maj. "I do remember his tendencies after so many orbits as his Eyes. But after his disgrace, I hoped he would learn to control those impulses. I know the First has similar thoughts," she answered.

"Thoughts not shared by the Chief. He knows the Seventh as well as any, and encourages him to raid," Maj spat back.

Orval-geeth shrugged. "Even the Chief's patience has its limits." She glanced at the timetracker mounted on the wall next to the portal. "When you hear from the Seventh, please remind him of the First's concerns. And let him know we look forward to inspecting his prize." She moved to exit the room, not waiting for any words Shurvil-maj might wish to add.

Descending to street level, the Eyes of the First lowered her brow to shield her eyes as a feeling of warmth ran through her. Things were all going to plan.

Shurvil-maj berated herself. She let the older female rattle her.

Maj knew that Orval-geeth held no attachment to Leeyak-dar. That female quickly landed with Sselmin-dor; almost at the moment the new First came to power. That Maj understood. But now it appeared that Geeth was actively working to block Dar's return to the higher ranks of the band.

And if Leeyak-dar's path was blocked, so was Maj's. That was unacceptable. The Voice of the Seventh didn't understand what reason Geeth had for doing this, but it didn't matter. Maj had to find a way to get around Orval-geeth's interference. Whatever it took.

Shad-var Swift-Raider Dominator
Over-space, en route to GC 46712-BLUE-2
1582:230:11:06:17 KT (2215SEP06 11:43 CUT)

Three nine-marks into their extended journey, Telrin-vak came to the Seventh's cabin, and after a moment to compose himself, pressed on the announcer. He felt a slight vibration from the control as the mechanism buzzed to alert the occupant and waited three breaths before the hatch rolled open.

"Come in, Master," Leeyak-dar ordered from the comfort of his nest. On seeing the look of concern on the Telrin-vak's face, he grudgingly climbed out. "Is there a problem?" he asked.

Vak stepped forward, holding out the data-plate he was carrying. "We have completed our translation of the information taken from the *hooman* slave. The system we travel to is not some minor outpost at the edge of their empire, as we first assumed. It is the closest star to their home star and likely heavily defended," he announced.

Dar took the device and skimmed through several screens of text; the legible Kray-ssass translation side-by-side with indecipherable scratchings that *hoomans* used to communicate. After a few *garm-voshtee* he looked up. "According to this, it is the companion star to our destination that is the primary settlement of the mammals. Our target star is home to only a small moon of the large gas world; a world among the inner rings. Fortunately, our destination is at the outer edge of this system."

The master was not soothed by this interpretation, arguing, "The risk is still considerable. We thought this world would be like the one we attacked with a force of ships, including *Silver Bounty*. If this information is true, we will be raiding a much stronger world with only a single ship."

"But we are not raiding the world, Master," Leeyak-dar reminded him. "We are raiding a distant moon at the far edge of that system. There will be no one in the area to notice our arrival." He brushed a symbol on the data-plate and brought up a diagram of the orbits of the various worlds around a trio of stars. "But your concern must be addressed. We will stay well clear of even the outer world and use the dark-skiff to approach our prize. This action will be nothing like the raids with *Silver Bounty*. *Dominator* must rely on stealth to take this first prize. Once we have a larger force, we can afford to take bold action." Dar waited until the master bent his neck in agreement. "Now, what else have you learned from the *hooman's* device?"

With his primary concern addressed, Telrin-vak adopted a leisurely stance. "As you told us, there are several eighteens of ships abandoned in this place, and it seems all are still functional. I cannot explain why the *hoomans* do this and the slave offers no explanation. Most are older hulls, but each one keeps its engines and weapons. It is a terrible waste simply to leave these to rot."

"These are aliens. Do not try to find reason in their actions," Leeyak-dar counseled.

Vak could not argue with that assessment, so he moved on to the question that really concerned him. "From this list, there are several haulers available, as well as larger attack ships. Why are we focused on this one small attacker when there are so many other choices? If we are to take only one ship, should it not be the largest?"

Leeyak-dar looked to his old comrade, then moved across the cabin to the small locker beside his nest. A flick of his tongue identified the Seventh and the locker hatch popped open. From inside, he extracted a small device. It was unlike the usual manufacture from the band's foundries, with a dull grey cover over most of the octagonal surface broken only by a black rectangle above a set of small grey buttons. Dar held the object up in one hand and explained, "Because of this. It is the key. With this, we can gain access to our prize and restart its systems."

Telrin-vak eyed the device suspiciously. "There was mention of codes in the text, but I assumed those were stored in a separate file. But this ... thing? It will only work with a single ship?"

The Seventh shrugged. "I assume. We know the slave used this to access our intended prize. It may work for others, but we cannot be certain."

"You spoke of stealing several ships. Eighteen or more," the old master exclaimed. "How can we do this? Are there more of these keys held somewhere? Do we just try this key on every ship until a hatch opens for us?"

"Be calm, Master," Leeyak-dar reassured the old male. "Once we have the first ship, it will explain how we can use this to take more of the others," he declared as he held out the device. "The first prize is not merely a test for us; it is a gate we must pass through to access the riches waiting for our grasp."

Despite those words, Telrin-vak was now more concerned about Leeyak-dar's plan than he was when he entered the cabin. "As you say, Seventh," he acquiesced, keeping his doubts to himself. From past experience, the old male knew when the time was right to question the actions of his superior, and this was not that time. Not yet at least.

Oblivious to the master's reservations, Leeyak-dar moved on to his own timetable. "What of your preparations? Have you assembled the prize crew?"

"From the description in the text, the controls should be similar to those found on the *hooman* hauler we captured in the past. Naymur-elv is studying the flying controls while the crafters will be ready to bring the power and drives to life. As long as the prize is of the same age as the hauler, I do not expect a problem." He paused before adding, "This assumes nothing has changed since the slave delivered the ship to this place."

Leeyak-dar shrugged at such concern. "These ships are unused; there is no reason for the *hoomans* to make any changes unless they plan to take these ships back into space. Do not seek out problems where none exist, Master. There are already more than enough to overcome," he advised.

Telrin-vak stretched out his neck in acquiescence. "We will still need raiders to take the ship with the steerer and crafters. Kalgun-dev has selected two to go with him; they will be shown how to aid the crafters to make the ship ready for travel." He was pleased when the Seventh voiced no objection to that plan, so he added as an afterthought, "and Choban-hath will join them to act as prize-master." It seemed like such an innocuous statement that Vak was surprised when Leeyak-dar responded.

"No," he declared flatly. When he saw the surprise in the master's eyes, he gave his reasoning, although no explanation was required of him. "Your steerer can be named prize-master; there is no reason to add another to the raid. The dark-skiff has place for only nine."

"And I send only nine, Seventh. Three crafters with the drive-master, two raiders with the raid-master, and the steerer. The overseer is the ninth," Yak enumerated. "Naymur-elv is a fine steerer, but she has no experience as a prize-master. This venture is too important to leave to one so young."

A bubbling sound came forth from the Seventh's crests, the Krayd equivalent of a chuckle. "Do not fear, old friend. I will properly supervise her ...."

Telrin-vak was stunned as he struggled to respond. "You? You intend to return in the prize? The risks are too great!" he blurted out.

"And that great risk is why I must do this," Leeyak-dar fired back. "Your own words - our steerer is too young. Too inexperienced. Well, no one on this swift raider has more experience in raids that I do." He paused a moment before admitting, "Except for you, of course. But I need you here in *Dominator*. Our ship is already under crewed, and we are sending a third to take the prize. I need you here to lead us back to Mid-port. "

Telrin-vak was unmoved. "It does not need to be you, Seventh. I can lead the raid if you think Choban-hath is unworthy. You do not need to take this risk."

"I must!" Leeyak-dar bellowed, snapping his jaw twice. His hand closed around the alien device he was holding and Telrin-vak thought for a moment the Seventh might crush it in his zeal. "I have the key to take the prize. I have studied the *hoomans* since our last raids orbits past; I understand them. I must be there to see that all is done to make this first raid a success, so that others can follow!" What Dar left unsaid was that he needed to be seen leading this raid in order to impress the Shad-var chief; deferring to underlings would not do in this case. And he could not afford another failure!

Telrin-vak surrendered to his superior's demands. "It will be as you say, Seventh."

JOHN LALLIER

CHAPTER 9

Shad-var Swift-Raider Dominator
Over-space, approaching GC 46712-BLUE-2
1582:297:09:00:05 KT (2215NOV12 05:53 CUT)

Travel through over-space was long and dull, as Leeyak-dar well knew. There were only so many times the raiders could train in the cargo holds or the crafters could practice their skills before the repetition numbed them. And only so many times the Seventh could read through the translations of the *hooman's* secret journal.

It was a male of its kind, and it had a name, though barely pronounceable to a speaker of Kray-ssass: *krew-noh-mah-rah-soh-vyk*. Stumbling through that odd combination of sounds brought discomfort to the Seventh's aural membranes and he went back to thinking of the mammal simply as 'the slave'. It just made everything easier for him.

The slave was only in the target ship for less than two nine-marks, ferrying the ship from one *hooman* port to another until it reached its final resting place. During that time, it made detailed plans on how it would return to the ship and take the vessel as its own. It included access and control codes, a catalog of items removed for storage and the locations for each as well as the minimum crew and skill set needed to carry out its plan. On first finding this information, a smirk crept onto Leeyak-dar's face as he almost admired the Krayd-like attention to detail the mammal displayed as it planned its 'raid'. The idea that a lower species was able to act in such a familiar and rational way surprised the Shad-var commander.

Still, for all its mimicry of intelligent thought, the *hooman* failed to anticipate the serious flaw in its scheme – the idea that it would be captured in someone else's raid. This was compounded when it attempted to barter for its freedom with the Krayd band that captured it. The very idea caused Dar to gurgle in laughter. How did it hope to trade its information for release when by rights the Krayd already owned everything they took from the prize ship, including this very journal. If such a ploy worked against its own kind, then *hoomans* were even less intelligent than Leeyak-dar first thought.

The Seventh turned off the plate and looked to the screen mounted across the cabin from his nest. On the panel, a faint green line attempted to mark out the path *Dominator* took from Garr-sum to their quarry. Only a *garm-liktee* remained until they reached their prize, and on the screen a mere scales thickness separated the green line from the purple star where all their preparations would be tested. Looking back towards Krayd space, the nearly straight path was betrayed by just two minor deviations.

At Telrin-vak's insistence, the swift raider made two stops at known Kray-da-like worlds along their journey to forage for stores. The master wanted to be certain that the prize crew took at least a nine-mark of packaged rations with them just in case the crew was unable to make use of the *hooman* supplies already inboard. He made this argument despite the Seventh insisting that the slave documented such precaution was unneeded.

"We cannot be certain that there is food still on the ship, and even if there it is, it may not be edible," Telrin-vak asserted at the time, a full four-ninths into their travel.

Leeyak-dar snapped his jaw at the concern. "That is preposterous. We already know that *hoomans* are edible. Why would the same not be true of whatever they themselves eat?"

Telrin-vak stubbornly stood by his concerns. "We cannot know what they eat; we only know what they eat when our slave masters feed them. For all we know, they might have nothing but plants on their ships for sustenance."

"Impossible," Leeyak-dar responded in frustration. "No species can hope to survive, much less ascend to the stars, on such a diet. Plants are not food; plants are what food eats!"

"These are aliens! You said as much yourself. We cannot know if the laws of the universe even apply to them," the old master argued back. "Whether there is food in the ship or not is not the question. If there is any chance that there is no food for the crew, we cannot risk foraging while still in the *hooman's* space. You need to take enough supplies to reach a world outside their grasp."

Much as Leeyak-dar wanted to argue with his master, the words caught in his throats as he considered them. Of all Krayd, Dar had too much experience of how the pesky mammals could quickly reduce even the best laid plans to utter chaos. Telrin-vak was not wrong to be cautious in this instance. Stretching out his neck as he shook his head he conceded, "Very well. I will allow one such delay to allow our raiders to hunt."

"Two," the old master countered. "We cannot be certain that a single hunt will provide enough game."

A low tone of anger simmered from the Seventh's crests as he replied, "Two then. But if these delays cost us our pride, the crew will be served your aged hide on the journey home!"

Telrin-vak wisely refrained from responding to that threat, largely because he was uncertain if the Seventh meant it figuratively or literally.

The first world *Dominator* visited appeared to put paid to the old master's fears. The raiders quickly found game in abundance and their trophies required three trips of the small lander to bring all of their many prizes to the swift raider. The crew feasted on flavorful meats that new-dark and for several to come. Given the raider's success, Leeyak-dar was ready to skip the second world altogether.

That might have been wise, since the second planet yielded no comparable bounty. The few animals the raiders were able to secure were scrawny, with tough leathery hides and little meat on the bones. This was just as well, since what flesh there was held a sour taste that no amount of spice could hide. Still, the crew availed themselves of this food for three rotations, though none enjoyed it, and all were happy to return to their flavorless rations at the appointed time.

After the long journey, Leeyak-dar was eager to dive into the work of raiding. He stepped into the control cabin moments before the ship returned to the universe once more.

"We emerge," Naymur-elv announced while on the screen the shimmering veil of under-space evaporated and the blackness once again enveloped *Dominator*. All those in the cabin basked in that view until an angry purple warning flashed on the screen. This was followed a breath later by a blue streak piercing the blackness as it shot towards the distant main star of this system.

"Activate the covert field!" Telrin-vak ordered as his monitors snapped to action. "Cut power to all scanners; silent detectors only!"

The Seventh moved forward to stand beside the swift raider's master. "What was that?" he demanded, though he feared he already knew the answer.

"A ship," Vak muttered as his eyes followed the faint pinpoint of blue light that was all that remained of the earlier bolt of lightning. Despite returning to the universe well beyond the reach of this system's thin shroud of rocks, *Dominator* was not alone out here. "It is possible we are already revealed," he added ominously. "Steerer, make hard move to left. Find us cover."

In his rage, Leeyak-dar nearly ripped the grab-bar from its overhead mounts. *How do the* hoomans *keep doing this?* he thought furiously. *Is it possible the old gods really are plotting against me?!*

Centauri Station
Sector 6, Alpha Centauri A IV (Cronus) orbit
2215NOV12 06:57 CUT

CRW1 Janco Smit was beginning to doze off at his station. He was nearly at the end of his shift and his replacement on alpha shift was due to relieve him in just over an hour. It couldn't come soon enough as far as Smit was concerned. Once again, the overnight shift in the operations center was dead, with little traffic moving about the system for the last seven hours. Most of the defense ships normally stationed around this system were off on maneuvers in the Wolf 359 system, while all the commercial operations were closed down for the night. Only two or three automated ore trains were moving across the system at this time.

A bleep from his console caught Smit off guard and he nearly spilled his coffee down the front of his teal uniform tunic as he sat upright. He tapped out a series of commands on the panel in front of him and called back to the officer on watch, "Lieutenant, I've got an unknown exiting drive-space. Bearing one-seven-five mark two down; range forty-two-point-three AU."

"Show me," LTJG Margarida Avila ordered as she hurried over to Smit's station. Despite her small stature, she bent slightly to peer over the crewman's shoulder as he highlighted the telltale numbers among a sea of data that first aroused the suspicion of the space station's computers. Avila took in this information, then called back, "Yeoman Lao, do we have any reported traffic?"

In a low voice, Smit added, "It's within range of Styx, ma'am. Maybe not close enough to set off the alarms, but still very close."

"I can see that, Crewman. Thank you," Avila returned while keeping her eyes on the display. She reached over Smit to tap a control and switch the image to a schematic of that section of the Alpha Centauri system. "Any update, Lao?" she called out as a reminder of her unanswered question.

The response was tentative. "Just confirming now, Lieutenant," a woman answered from the far corner of the chamber. As Avila turned around to spot the speaker from across the room, Lao followed in a louder voice, "Confirmed. A Tyndal medium trader out of Labrel. Registered as RK:23-27:18; they came in short of their intended entry point. Proceeding to the ore processing plant on Tartarus."

Avila shook her head in disbelief at the explanation. "All right. Forward that report to the Celestial Administration and let's make sure that ship updates its charts before departure. A couple of AU's further off course and they would have been in real trouble." Margarida could only imagine the havoc that would have resulted from the Tyndal freighter popping back into real space in the middle of the Fleet storage zone that trailed Styx around the system. Not to mention the amount of datawork that would have fallen on her if that disaster happened during gamma shift.

Smit spun his chair slightly to look up to the officer still standing behind him. "Lieutenant, should I flag the incident for review?"

Avila considered that for a moment but then shook her head. "You heard the petty officer; we already know it was the Tyndal freighter. Mystery solved. There's no reason to bother the commodore with this."

Avila was already walking back to her console as Smit replied, "Yes, ma'am." With a swipe of his hand, he cleared the information from his display and reset the system to go back to its usual routine. As he looked up from his station, he noticed a new entry added to the large overhead display that dominated the operations center. The short orange line quickly turned green, then stretched out in an arc to reach towards one of the numerous moons of the enormous gas giant that their space station orbited.

With a sigh, Janco glanced at the chronometer. *Only forty-nine minutes to go.*

Shad-var Swift-Raider Dominator
GC 46712-BLUE-2, 44 AU from primary
1582:297:11:14:02 KT (2215NOV12 09:14 CUT)

For two *garm-liktee Dominator* huddled in the shadows of a rock only slightly larger than the swift raider itself, waiting for some *hooman* ship to come out and challenge it. But no ship arrived and Telrin-vak finally turned towards Leeyak-dar. "We can sense no vessel targeting our location. What little movement exists is directed towards the gas world deep in this system's inner circles. It appears we have avoided detection."

Leeyak-dar was less certain as he demanded, "How? That ship passed within range of our guns. How did it not see us and report our presence?"

Vak shrugged. "Perhaps it was a hauler; these are not known to have sharp eyes. If it was focused on its path, it could fail to notice us unless we forced it to alter direction to avoid impact."

"Even mammals have eyes," Dar tossed back, unconvinced. "We cannot rely on good luck to hide us from every ship in this system."

"There are few of those," the master countered. "It is odd; from the records there should be many heavy fighting ships defending the inner reaches of this system. But our detectors can find only two, and both are tied to the large waystation at the gas world." He paused for a moment before asking, "Where are the rest now? Raiding?"

Leeyak-dar waved a claw. "Or whatever the *hoomans* do in place of such sport. Doubtless they have a reason for building such ships." He moved forward towards the main screen, studying the mix of purple and grey objects rendered. "Whatever the reason, we must make use of this good fortune. We will move on our target before their ships return."

"As you say, Seventh," Telrin-vak readily agreed. "*Dominator* can move to a closer position while keeping beyond the view of their detectors. We will release the dark-skiff once we are in range; I will alert Kalgun-dev and Elldor-min to prepare their teams." He turned to face the pilot station. "Steerer, take us towards the prize, and find a suitable rock to use as cover. Stalking speed."

"Stalking speed," Naymur-elv confirmed and within breaths a slight rumble ran through the deck plates as the swift raider turned towards its quarry.

Shad-var Swift-Raider Dominator
GC 46712-BLUE-2, 40 AU from primary
1582:297:16:14:17 KT (2215NOV12 16:17 CUT)

It was approaching mid-dark when the swift raider came to rest approximately one-eighteenth *zel-hosh* from a smallish grey world. Above that world, a minor waystation hung – the only source of energy in this distant corner of the otherwise unremarkable twin-sun system. Between the swift raider and the station, an assortment of alien ships drifted along. Naymur-elv was careful to keep the bulk of those hulls between *Dominator* and the *hooman* station. With luck, even if the swift raider appeared on the alien's screens, they would assume it was one of the numerous ships they already knew about.

Leeyak-dar ate sparingly at the last feeding in his cabin; despite the possibility of short rations once they were on the prize, he could not bring himself to indulge with his last meal inboard *Dominator*. The Seventh's earlier bravado was absent as he prepared for his first active raid in many orbits. In all the time when Dar was First of Shad-var, he directed the actions of others from the comfort of *Silver Bounty*. This-mark he was headed into the breach with a blaster held high.

Halfway down the spine of ship, he spotted Kalgun-dev doublechecking equipment at the hatch to the hold, tapping at a data-plate with gloved hands. Since they knew the life systems on the target ship were turned off, the raid-master was decked out in a dark grey battle-suit, the helmet hanging from a hook on one hip while his blaster dangled on the opposite side. The sight left Leeyak-dar feeling self-conscious of the basic air-suit he was wearing, a simple sheath with none of the armor plates or covert appearance of the raider's attire. Dar consoled himself with the knowledge that their target was unguarded and the precautions taken by the raid-master would prove unnecessary. At least, the Seventh hoped it would be so.

Kalgun-dev finally noticed Leeyak-dar and spoke up. "Seventh, our master has overloaded the skiff. Most of the rations will need to be brought over in a second crossing," he informed his superior as he gestured to a pile of crates still waiting in the connectway. "I will send one of our raiders to retrieve this once we have cleared the prize of traps."

Dar almost smirked at the remark. "Do you really believe the *hoomans* have left traps for us?" he wondered aloud.

Kalgun-dev shrugged and answered, "I always expect the worst. This way, I am ready when I find it." He placed the data-plate on the pile of crates and moved into the hold. The Seventh followed him.

Two more raiders were waiting inside, both dressed as Kalgun-dev in dark grey battle suits, though on these two the material looked well worn, with numerous dents and scorches from previous boardings. Unfortunately, the males in those suits were not nearly as experienced as their attire made them appear; Leeyak-dar knew the battle suits were salvaged from the band's better provisioned ships that could afford to replace items when they became faulty.

Dar moved past the raiders and skirted around the side of the skiff to reach the forward hatch. Stepping inside, he found the rest of his prize crew. The steerer, Naymur-elv, was busying herself at the controls of the small craft, while behind her Elldor-min and her crafters were securing their gear to the back wall of the skiff. "Do you have everything you will need, Drive-master?" he asked to get the attention of the group.

Like Dar, Elldor-min was attired in a basic air-suit, the mask dangling just below her snout. At the sound of her commander, she spun about and tried to bring herself to an appropriate stance. "We have all we can carry, Seventh," she answered. "But until we see the *hooman* machines, we cannot know if we have everything we will need."

This was not the reassurance Leeyak-dar was looking for so close to his prize, and his displeasure was evident in his tone. "And what do you plan to do if you find you lack some vital tool, Drive-master? You cannot have one of your crafters scamper back to *Dominator* for the missing item!"

The old female was not cowed by the Seventh's response. She shrugged and answered, "I assume the *hoomans* have tools designed to service their machines. We will simply make use of those." She didn't wait for Dar's reply and turned back to supervise her crafters.

Leeyak-dar glanced to the side to spot the steerer decidedly focused on her screen despite being well within hear-length of the previous exchange. Dar appreciated that the young female knew better than to comment and so chose to let the matter pass. He moved to sit on the bench across the center aisle from the steerer's station on the right side of the craft and ordered, "Make ready to launch."

"All inboard now!" Naymur-elv announced and in moments the three raiders piled into the craft, with their master closing the hatch behind him. Unlike the others in the skiff who occupied the six benches, the three raiders stood in the well in front of the steerer's station, securing themselves with cables that attached to their belts while grasping the handholds above. With a gesture from Dev, the steerer declared, "All inboard, Seventh."

Dar shook his head in approval before ordering, "Clear the hold of air; open cargo hatch."

"As you say," Elv replied dutifully and stabbed at the controls on her panel. It took a few breaths before a vibration ran through the deck betraying the fact that the massive doors to the cargo hold were opening to space. Since there were no windows along the side of the dark skiff, the only visual evidence was what was shown on Naymur-elv's screen. When the vibrations finally ceased, she announced, "Cargo hatch open."

Leeyak-dar took a calming breath before replying, "Take us to our prize, steerer." A tingle ran through Dar's jaw and his tongue flicked. Despite the stale canned air of the skiff, the Seventh was certain he could feel the scent of blood. *Victory is finally within my grasp*, he mused as his left hand closed around the imaginary *hooman* ship his mind projected.

CHAPTER 10

Shad-var Dark-skiff
GC 46712-BLUE-2, 40 AU from primary
1582:297:17:09:02 KT (2215NOV12 17:11 CUT)

Leeyak-dar sat in silence as the dark-skiff slowly carried them across the blackness of space to their destination, and as a result the others followed their leader's example. After what Dar was certain was an eternity, Naymur-elv finally announced. "Eighty-one *zel-kray* from the prize, Seventh. I can see the hatch that was shown on the maps; shall I approach?" she asked.

"Yes," Dar answered automatically, then added, "Release the mimic here, then bring us beside." He leaned over on his bench hoping to steal a glance of the steerer' screen. Unfortunately, the only things visible were a set of diagrams and a series of numbers that probably were of great value to the small craft's pilot but meant nothing to Leeyak-dar. Given that, he satisfied himself with waiting for the gentle thump that indicated when the skiff came into contact with the prize's hull.

Elv's head swiveled several times as she checked and rechecked the numbers on her screen before proclaiming, "We are hard against the hull; the hatch is straight ahead."

"Seal helmets; pump out the air," Kalgun-dev ordered from the forward hatch as he moved to face their destination. Even the Seventh jumped at the sound of that command, fixing his mask in place before activating the suit's air processor. He noted the gauge on his sleeve that showed he had a four *garm-liktee* supply of atmosphere, with an additional two *garm-liktee* available in the spare bottle. If Elldor-min was unable to restart the prize's environment systems in that time, Dar and the others would have to return to the skiff to refill their containers.

Without looking back to check that the prize crew followed his order, the raid-master reached out to the control at the side of the hatch. With a solid yank down on the lever, the skiff's hatch rolled to the side as a gentle rush of remaining air swirled the small amount of dust on the skiff's deck. This revealed a second hatch, this one colored in sickly blood-white that caused a brief shudder to run down the Seventh's spine. For a moment, he'd forgotten that the pink-skinned *hoomans* chose to drape their ships in this peculiar color, rather than the pale blue of their more common, blue-skinned fellows. While neither was attractive by Krayd standards, this specific shade always made Leeyak-dar think of the blood-soaked floors of a slaughterhouse.

He was pulled from these thoughts when Kalgun-dev spun around and announced, "Seventh. We need your access codes to open this hatch."

In the light gravity and vacuum of the skiff, Leeyak-dar rose and stepped carefully forward until he was within reach of the alien portal. Pulling the device from a belt pouch, he held the alien machine out until it was nearly in contact with the white surface of the portal before tapping awkwardly at controls designed for alien hands. Entering the foreign symbols he memorized earlier, he was rewarded as a blue light on the device turned green. There was a slight delay and for a moment Leeyak-dar feared all the faith he put in the information he purchased on Garr-sum was in vain, but eventually the hatch slid to the side to reveal a dark chamber.

Kalgun-dev shouldered past Dar and the other two raiders quickly followed their leader into the void. After a nine-count, the raid-master called out, "There is a second portal; this is an air chamber."

"Do you require the access device again?" the Seventh asked as he moved forward to join the raiders. Unlike the raiders, his air-mask did not allow him to see in the darkened chamber nor did his boots allow him to adhere to the deck of the alien ship. Dar activated the light attached to his left sleeve as he floated into the weightless space. Playing the beam about him he was confronted by more white walls, broken occasionally by labels and markers in the unfamiliar symbols *hoomans* used.

"No, Seventh," Kalgun-dev answered as he reached out to the recessed hatch across the chamber from the skiff. His gloved hand probed a panel beside the hatch and on the third attempt the second hatch slid aside much as the first had. "It appears they do not lock the inner portal," Dev observed, and he gestured for one of the raiders to precede him into the ship.

Leeyak-dar floated over to the now open portal, noticing for the first time the lack of hand grabs in the *hooman* air chamber. He wondered how they handled the lack of gravity in this space, noting that the decking in this space was clad in the same stark white as the walls, while the corridor on the other side of the portal revealed a less noxious palette. The walls and ceiling (assuming the Krayd correctly identified 'up' on this alien ship) were a dull but pleasing grey while the deck was covered in a bluish material reminiscent of untanned *chutar* hide. There appeared to be a metal under that fabric as Kalgun-dev walked up to the Seventh, the soles of his boots adhering to the floor despite the absence of gravity.

"From the markings, this is the third level," the raid-master began before pointing down the darkened corridor. "According to the maps provided, the connectway at the next junction should lead to the drive chamber. We will need to go up two levels to reach the control cabin."

Leeyak-dar considered this, then glanced back to the light coming in from the skiff still attached to the outer portal. Naymur-elv was venturing into the air chamber with Elldor-min right behind her. "The two raiders will lead the drive-master and her crafters to the drive chamber; they need to restore power and life systems as quickly as possible," Dar declared on the common channel. He didn't wait for a response before adding, "I will take the raid-master and steerer to the control cabin. Once we have power, we need to get this ship moving."

Naymur-elv moved towards the commander, commenting, "It is possible that restoring power will alert the *hoomans* to our presence."

Dar pulled a coil of line from his belt and attached the hook on the end to a corresponding loop on the female's belt. "Then you will need to work quickly, steerer. I don't intend to be here when they come looking for their missing ship."

It took three *garm-maltee* for the trio to maneuver through the ship. With no handholds along the corridors, Kalgun-dev was forced to tow Leeyak-dar and Naymur-elv as they floated since only Dev had any traction on the decking. Things improved in the two ladderways, where all three were able to push themselves up the rungs. When they finally reached the hatch to the control cabin, they encountered their first obstacle since entering the ship. Once again, Dar's alien device was required to unlock the portal and grant them access.

The control cabin had the layout of a stunted triangle, with a large screen running across the top blocking access to the point. Set back from that were two freestanding consoles with what could be a stool at each, with a third stool located behind those in the center of the cabin. To either side were consoles mounted to the walls. As with the rest of the ship, there were no handholds along any of the surfaces, and the ceiling of the chamber was far too high to mount any.

Leeyak-dar detached from his companions and gently floated towards the center stool, grabbing its high back to prevent himself from impacting the screen. Righting himself, he examined the furnishings, noting the devices mounted to the sides of this one stool that set it apart from the others. He also noticed the closed back and odd contours of the seat, something obviously not designed to accommodate the tail stump of a Krayd. "This will have to be replaced with a proper bench. But for now, at least it gives us something to hold onto," he commented.

While he was inspecting the chair, Naymur-elv skirted the cabin and came to rest at one of the two forward consoles. "One of these should be the steerer's station, but which one? And what does the other one do?" she asked.

"Gunner's station most likely," Kalgun-dev replied without turning away from his inspection of their surroundings. "What I can't identify is this," he continued as he stared at a metallic rectangle mounted to the dull grey wall by the portal. "It doesn't look like a control for anything. But it's covered in glyphs."

Reluctantly, Leeyak-dar pushed himself over to join the raid-master, grabbing the male's arm in lieu of a handhold. Spotting the object of the Kalgun-dev's curiosity, he pulled his translation screen from a belt pouch and steadied it on the item in question. After a time, the image on the screen was replaced with proper text. "It is a sign, but many of the symbols do not translate to Kray-ssass. Some of it talks of ships and shipyards and construction, but the rest must be *hooman* names of places or people.

"What do the large symbols say?" the steerer asked after joining them at the rear of the cabin.

"A-LE-ZAN'DE-RE," Dar answered, stumbling through the jumble of letters on his screen. "Perhaps the name of the band that built this ship."

"An unfortunate name then. Their vessel is so easily taken," the steerer remarked. "And for names, have you chosen one for your new prize, Seventh?"

Leeyak-dar gurgled slightly at the young female's question. He had planned to wait until the ship was under way as was custom but decided that revealing this one item early would not lead to misfortune. "Yes. Naymur-elv, you are now prize-master of *Emerald Dagger*. I suggest as your first act, you contact the drive-master and find out when we will have power. Only then can you make a path for home."

Despite the lack of gravity, Naymur-elv bounced up to stand taller while grasping the edge of the console next to her. "Yes, Seventh. It will be as you say," she answered loudly.

Shad-var Prizeship Emerald Dagger (nee CSS Alexander)
GC 46712-BLUE-2, 40 AU from primary
1582:298:04:03:15 KT (2215NOV12 23:27 CUT)

Over four *garm-liktee* later (*nearly a quarter rotation!*), Leeyak-dar was still floating in the dark of the control cabin. Once again, his eyes were drawn to the gauge that measured his air supply. The crew were forced to switch to their spare bottles seven *garm-maltee* earlier and right now one of the raiders was refilling the main bottles from the skiff's air supply. But that would be the last extension the crew could afford. If the crafters were unable to restore power to the ship's life systems, they would have no choice but to return to *Dominator. I cannot afford another failure!* Dar's mind screamed as his claws dug into the back of the chair he was using as an anchor.

To calm himself, Dar checked through the few successes they had so far. Since they boarded the abandoned ship, Kalgun-dev was able to locate the components from the ship's main guns that had been removed and locked away by the hooman when the ship first arrived. Taking advantage of the current lack of gravity the raid-master and one of his raiders moved the containers back to the forward weapons space and were now working on restoring the guns to working order. At least, once the power was restored.

The other raider returned from *Dominator* with the skiff some time ago, bringing with him the bulk of their provisions. The containers were now stacked in the corridor outside the air chamber where the skiff waited to either depart or return the crew to the swift raider. A part of Dar would rather end his existence than do the latter.

And through trial and error, Naymur-elv believed she had found a suitable manual setting for the chairs at each of the control cabin's consoles. Of course, they would not know for certain until the simulated gravity was powered. Exhaling slowly, Leeyak-dar ticked the control for his radio. "Drive-master, report progress?" he demanded.

The voice of the old female sounded just as tired as Leeyak-dar felt. "It is unchanged, Seventh. The drive systems remain locked. Your codes are working but must be reentered at each panel as we go through the steps to bring the reactors to full power."

Dar snorted. "So, no change since the last report!" he fired back angrily. *This is all Telrin-vak's fault; his promise that this female could work any drive is proving to be a lie!* "Our air will not last forever, crafter. You must power the life systems now."

Elldor-min didn't back down from the implied demotion in her status. "We can power life systems now, plus others like communications and detectors. But that will probably alert the *hoomans* to our presence," she reminded the Seventh.

"We must risk it," Dar replied, recalling the first rule of raiding – he who risks is rewarded. All ventures involve risk; it is up to the leader to know when that risk is worth the prize. And when it is not. Leeyak-dar didn't become First by avoiding risk, and he wasn't going to regain his former position by shying away now.

Unlike the Seventh, Elldor-min did not believe in risk; no crafter did. Things either worked or they did not. Taking risks was a sure way to guarantee the latter. "One more *garm-liktee*, Seventh," she pleaded. "Probably less. That is all we need now."

Leeyak-dar looked to the gauge on his sleeve. "It had better be less for your sake, Drive-master," he growled and then ended the call.

The lights in the control cabin flickered on in half the allotted time, and Leeyak-dar felt himself being gently pulled down to the blue-colored deck as gravity slowly returned. "Our drive-master is true to her word," he declared, and casually lifted the mask away from his face. A flick of his tongue provided a quick assessment. The air was stale, which was to be expected; they had no idea how long the system had been dormant, and it would be some time before the whole ship was livable. The priority now was the control cabin and the drive chamber; the rest could wait until they were on their way home.

Leeyak-dar took a step away from the chair he had been grasping and stumbled. As he righted himself, he noticed that he felt the weight of the device in his hand more than when he'd been on *Dominator*. He ticked the radio once more. "Drive-master, the gravity has returned but is it correct?"

"It is correct for *hoomans*, Seventh. We are working to make it proper for us," Elldor-min returned, the weariness masking any anger in her voice. "I regret that such adjustments may take some time to control."

Dar recognized that his comment came off as criticism and corrected course. "It is no matter; we will learn to adapt for now. Focus your crafters on the drive."

"At once, Seventh," Min replied and ended the call.

Leeyak-dar gurgled at the affront but let it pass; he was happy to finally extract himself from the air-suit and wasn't going to let a little insubordination ruin his mood. The prize was his!

"Seventh," Naymur-elv broke his brief reverie as she called his attention to the console in front of her. Perching on the edge of the chair, her hands swept over the image on the screen that occupied the center of the console. "This is the steerer position, but I am also able to access the main detectors from this screen," she explained, and with a touch of her claw the image on the screen changed. It now showed a sea of blue dots, each with tiny *hooman* glyphs next to the dot. "There are over fifty-four ships out there, all of them essentially motionless as seen from our position while the swarm orbits the star. All except one," she declared, and the image zoomed in to focus on a cluster of dots. One indeed was making a slow transit across the image while the others were stationary.

"One of the ships is moving. Towards us?" Leeyak-dar asked as he watched the screen.

The neophyte prize-master ducked her head. "This cannot tell me. I would need to activate scanners, and that would certainly get their attention." She paused before delivering yet more bad news, "There is a second reason for concern. The ship we are on is calling out to some other ship or base nearby."

Leeyak-dar pulled his data-plate out and flipped through its contents. "Yes," he answered idly. "It has been since before we entered. I believe it is an automatic reply to the owners of the ship that it is in its proper place. The mimic we released has been monitoring and recording the signal." On the screen, he rolled through the data collected by the small device the skiff dropped in space before connecting to the prize. "It does not appear that there is any change since we opened the air chamber, nor since the drive-master restored power." With a grunt, he turned off the plate and returned it to its pouch. "Nevertheless, we cannot ignore your moving ship."

Dar moved away from Naymur-elv to stand by the chair he planned to use. "Raid-master, have your male move the skiff into the hold of this ship. We are leaving."

With his helmet removed, Kalgun-dev whistled softly as his head bobbed before speaking into the microphone on the collar of his battle suit. "Norshel-gat, move the skiff to the doors of the cargo hold. I will meet you there." He reseated the helmet of his battle suit as he passed through the hatch – there was no way of knowing if the route to the hold was already pressurized.

The Seventh turned to Elv once more. "Prize-master, find us a path home," he instructed.

CHAPTER II

CSV Brookhaven
Sector 6, Alpha Centauri AB XII (Styx) orbit, 40 AU from primary
2215NOV13 00:16 CUT

The lights on the bridge of the gunboat *Brookhaven* were dim given the late hour. In less than six hours their four-day patrol would come to an end when their sistership, *Huntington*, was scheduled to relieve them. Given that, the last watch of the patrol fell to the ship's executive officer. ENS Beren Özdemir was just getting comfortable at the helm when the crewman at the comms station interrupted her routine.

"XO, request from Styx Center. They are getting some strange readings from section seven," the man reported.

Özdemir waited for the crewman to continue, then sighed. "That's not a request, Basco," she pointed out.

The nineteen-year-old crewman seemed confused. "Yes, ma'am. Uh. No, ma'am ... I mean ... I think they want us to check it out," he stammered.

Beren turned in her seat to face the bewildered crewman. "You think?" she asked with a touch of concern. CRW2 Basco wasn't normally this incompetent and she chalked it up to a mixture of boredom and fatigue at the end of the patrol.

Basco quickly corrected his earlier statement. "No, ma'am. They ... they definitely want us to check it out."

The XO eyed the crewman suspiciously, then pressed, "And was this an urgent request?"

Recognizing his earlier uncertainty, Basco corrected course. "No, ma'am. Just want us to know the situation, and asked if we could check it out," he pronounced firmly.

Özdemir turned back to the console and brought up the chart. The Centauri Storage Zone was a sphere roughly two hundred thousand kilometers in radius around a central anchor beacon orbiting the type E3 planet Styx at twice that distance. Every ship assigned to the zone was assigned a unique distance and vector from the anchor so that the group maintained spacing as they collectively orbited the planet. *Brookhaven* normally circled the zone at a leisurely pace once every two hours, altering her course at each circuit to cover most of the sphere. One thing they never did was go through the zone – that would play havoc on the automated systems of the nearly sixty unmanned ships within. And at the moment, section seven was on the opposite of the sphere from the gunboat's position.

The executive officer stared at the display for a moment, then shrugged. "Oh, what the hell. We can increase speed," she admitted aloud. After making an adjustment to the controls she announced, "ETA thirty-four minutes."

At the comms station, Basco nodded. "I will let Styx Center know. Should I also inform the captain?" he asked sincerely.

Again, Özdemir turned in her seat to stare at the man. "Why? Are you looking for a demotion, Crewman?" she asked with a smile, hoping Basco would take the words in the spirit she intended. "It's probably nothing. It's definitely not worth waking the captain over." She turned back in her chair to focus on the image of space on the main display. "There's no reason for anyone to panic just yet."

Shad-var Prizeship Emerald Dagger (nee CSS Alexander)
GC 46712-BLUE-2, 40 AU from primary
1582:298:04:17:15 KT (2215NOV13 00:29 CUT)

"That ship is moving faster now, Seventh. It will reach us sooner," Naymur-elv informed her commander. "Perhaps six *garm-maltee*," she added after poking buttons on the console.

Finally free of his air-suit, Leeyak-dar tapped the radio attached to his collar. "Drive-master, we need to depart now!"

The husky voice of the old female responded through the tinny speakers of the radio. "We are close, Seventh. Another seven *garm-maltee* and we will be ready," Elldor-min answered.

"You have five!" Dar fired back. "A *hooman* ship approaches and I do not plan to be here when it arrives!" The sound of the hatch opening caught him off guard and he watched as a young crafter stepped through the portal. "What is this?" he demanded.

The crafter froze in place and looked up, startled. "I … I … I am sent to turn off the radio. I must do it from that panel," the young female stammered. She raised a tentative hand to point to the console on the left-side wall of the cabin.

Leeyak-dar was fuming as he studied the child, dressed still in her air-suit. Before he could demand a better explanation, Elldor-min spoke up from his collar-radio. "That is Mayvel-ahn, Seventh. She is there at my instruction," the drive-master clarified.

"Why is she not with you, preparing the drive?" Dar demanded.

A short sigh escaped the drive-master's throat and was picked up by the radio. "She works the life systems and the data systems, including the radio. Ahn does not work the drives," Elldor-min expounded, trying with limited success to avoid the tone of a lecturer.

"Fine," Dar growled then waved an accusing hand from the wayward crafter to the console she sought. "A message escapes this ship; it must be silenced before we can move. Be quick!" he ordered.

"It will be done, Seventh," Mayvel-ahn bleated, then scampered across the control cabin to her destination, fearing any delay would lead to repercussions not to be considered. The crafters rarely had an opportunity to deal with the commander, and so feared the worst from him.

Snapping his jaw in frustration, Leeyak-dar reminded the drive-master, "You have four *garm-maltee*!" He closed the connection and was ready to return to Naymur-elv's side when the radio buzzed again. "What, Raid-master?" he demanded, knowing there was only one person remaining to speak with.

"Seventh, we are not able to open the cargo hold doors. The drive-master cannot spare anyone to find the fault," Kalgun-dev informed his commander.

A deep bass tone rose up from Leeyak-dar's crest as he fumed over yet another obstacle in his path. Snapping his jaw, he barked out, "There is no time. Have your raider return to the air chamber; we must abandon the skiff." The plan had been to hide the theft of

Emerald Dagger for as long as possible, but it now seemed that was impossible. His best hope now was to distract the *hoomans* while he escaped with his prize.

"As you say, Seventh," Kalgun-dev agreed. "Norshel-gat, return to the air chamber. Remove anything of value from the skiff and release it. You have two *garm-liktee*," he ordered.

A second voice joined in. "Yes, Raid-master. Should I set the destruct charge?"

"No," Leeyak-dar answered in place of his raid-master. The more he thought about it, losing the skiff might come back to taint his victory and he would not risk that. It might still be possible for the swift raider to retrieve the skiff after *Emerald Dagger* escaped. "Set the skiff to return to *Dominator,* but do not activate the beacon. That should allow it to avoid the *hoomans'* detectors."

"You have your orders," Kalgun-dev added and the raider aboard the skiff chimed off. "Seventh, we will return to work on the guns."

"Let us hope we do not need them," Leeyak-dar answered before tapping the radio off. He moved to stand over Mayvel-ahn at the communications console. "Crafter, have you mastered the ship's radio?" he demanded.

The female looked up as her much taller commander towered over her and nervously ducked her head in obedience. "It is ready, Seventh. I need only enter the final instruction."

Dar sneered in delight and pulled the data-plate from his pouch once more. With his claw hovering over the screen he instructed, "Do it now!" At the same time, he punched down on his device to activate the mimic's true function. That done, he studied the symbols that appeared on the screen for a moment before shoving the device back into its pouch with a satisfied shake of his head. Returning his attention to Mayvel-ahn, he instructed, "This is your station now; master it. We must use this radio to contact *Dominator,* and I do not want the *hoomans* to be aware of our actions. See to that, crafter."

He turned away without waiting for a response and Ahn gave a brief tone of relief that she hoped the commander would ignore.

Moving back to Naymur-elv's side, Dar asked, "Do we have a working drive yet, Prize-master?"

The steerer looked to her console but to no avail. "No, Seventh," she admitted dejectedly before adding, "but the drive-master still has time."

"Less time than she knows," Dar countered. He stared at the large screen before him; it was currently focused on an image of a second hooman ship drifting along with *Emerald Dagger* in its circle of the tiny nearby planet. "Move the ship. Even if it is only the gas thrusters. We need to be away from this place before that other ship arrives."

Naymur-elv cocked her head to the side as she considered the order but decided she had no choice but to comply. She might be prize-master in name, but Leeyak-dar was still the one in charge and she could not question his commands as Telrin-vak might. Instead, she answered, "As you say," and tapped out instructions on the console. After a moment, the image of the second ship began to slide slowly to the left.

CSV Brookhaven
Sector 6, Alpha Centauri AB XII (Styx) orbit, 40 AU from primary
2215NOV13 00:43 CUT

Özdemir looked up from her display in confusion, then tapped out a series of commands. On the main display, a series of blue markers appeared with small blocks of text next to each – one marker for each of the nine ships in this section of the storage zone. The executive officer silently studied the information presented, double-checking the information on her console more than once. After a time, she shook her head and tapped a button. "Captain, please report to the bridge," she asked with mild regret. Beren had hoped to spare her commanding officer the interruption to his well-earned rest.

Ninety seconds later, the doors to the bridge opened and LT Midthunder strode through. He was dressed in his low gravity jumpsuit (doubtless because his standard duty uniform was in the auto-valet at the moment) and his normally straight black hair was disheveled. "What do we have, XO?" he asked as he moved to stand beside his usual chair in the center of the room.

Beren groaned inwardly as the one who woke the captain, but that was done now, and nothing could change that. "We had a report from Styx Center of unusual readings from section seven. I moved us into position to investigate and it looks like they were correct. I show at least four ships out of position," the XO reported.

Midthunder dropped into his chair and wondered aloud, "Four ships? It's odd to have even one ship out of place, but four?" He ran his hand over his head, momentarily restoring order to his hair as he thought. "What ships?" he asked, peering at the image on the main display.

Özdemir tapped a control and four of the blue markers became brighter. "*New York*, *Yamamoto*, *Alexander* and *Saladin*," she answered.

"A destroyer and three frigates," the captained summarized as he looked down. "Why couldn't it be one of the freighters?" he grumbled to himself before popping back up to ask, "I suppose it's possible the beacon is the problem. It might be sending out bad instructions. Did Styx Center run a diagnostic of the system?"

Özdemir looked back sheepishly, confessing, "I didn't ask. I mean, I assume they did – there would be no reason to contact us if they didn't already check their own equipment." Even as she said it, the words sounded more like a question of her own actions than an indictment of the base personnel at Styx Center.

The young captain of the gunboat wasn't looking to place blame. He looked over his shoulder to the crewman at the comms station. "Basco, contact the center. Check with them that someone actually tested the beacon before sending us on this hunt. And get someone up here to take the ops station." Leaning forward, he addressed his next order to Özdemir. "Ensign, take us in a little closer. I want a better view of those ships."

Six minutes later, Midthunder was standing beside CPO Atticus as she studied the central display on her console. "I can't explain it, Captain. But the sensors cannot find her."

Midthunder shook his head. "And yet the transponder says she is right where she is supposed to be," he countered, though admitting, "more or less," in a lower voice.

The old Roman non-com just shrugged at his reply. "What can I tell you, Captain? I don't know what transponder you're tracking, but the sensors don't lie. There's no ship at those coordinates. None." She spun in her chair after making her pronouncement. "Unless the ship is cloaked somehow, and we can't see her. But as far as I know, the Commonwealth doesn't have cloaking technology and even if we did, why would we put it on an obsolete frigate?" With more years under her belt than her commanding officer, Atticus gave the young officer a wry look. "We don't have cloaking tech, do we Captain?"

Midthunder fought to keep a grin from forming, answering, "Not to my knowledge, Chief. But you never know." He turned to look at the main display. "Well, if the ship isn't where it says it is, where the hell is it? Run a full sensor sweep, all directions. If that frigate is drifting, it couldn't have gotten very far since our last pass yesterday." He moved back towards his chair.

Atticus set to work at her console. "How far out do you want to look, sir?" she asked.

"Five hundred megameters. If we still can't find it, take it out another five hundred," he answered with equal nonchalance. "Then make it two thousand. But it has to be out there somewhere!"

Shad-var Prizeship Emerald Dagger (nee CSS Alexander)
GC 46712-BLUE-2, 40.1 AU from primary
1582:298:05:03:07 KT (2215NOV13 00:45 CUT)

Leeyak-dar was breathing easier with *Emerald Dagger* now under power and moving towards the point where they could activate the ship's FTL drive. Assuming, of course, that the drive-master was able to get the horrible thing working.

"I am grateful to have the near-space drive, master. But we are still in peril if you cannot bring our sphere-drive to power," he reminded Elldor-min once again. He debated donning his air-suit again and going down to the drive chamber, but finally decided against it. *They will not complete the task any faster if I stand over them with a shock-rod*, he reminded himself.

"If it were a sphere-drive, it would be working now, Seventh," the drive-master replied. "But the bizarre contraption the *hoomans* built defies description. Fortunately, it is powered by its own furnaces, or even the near-space drive would be denied us."

Leeyak-dar seethed and desperately wanted to lash out at ... someone. Anyone. Like any senior member of the band, feeling powerless was worse than death. At least death could be fought. But he held his tongue. "Bizarre or not, you must beat that drive into submission. We cannot escape without it."

Elldor-min was no less frustrated than her commander. "Do not worry, Seventh. I will find a way to start this primitive drive, even if I have to strip away half of these parts. I go now," she declared and dropped the connection.

The Seventh's reprieve from disaster was brief. Naymur-elv looked up from the screen she was studying. "That ship is now probing the space nearby. They have not detected us yet, but it is only a matter of time," she informed Leeyak-dar.

The commander thought quickly, then ordered, "The time for deception has passed. The moment you believe they have found us, bring our drive to its highest speed. How far are we now from our pursuer?"

The prize-master snorted. "Less than a ninth of a *zel-hosh*, Seventh. At our present speed, even the dark-skiff is leaving us far behind. It is half the distance to *Dominator*."

"No one is chasing the skiff, Prize-master," he reminded the female before moving towards Kalgun-dev, who hovered in the background. "Raid-master, I need you to take the gunner's station," he declared, waving an arm to the place to the right of Naymur-elv.

Kalgun-dev was taken aback. "Seventh, I am a raider, not a gunner," he protested.

"You know how to wield a weapon; wield this one," Dar insisted. He blamed himself for not bringing a trained gunner on the raid, but then consoled himself. *Dominator* had only the one gunner and he was needed on the swift raider more than *Emerald Dagger*. There, at least, he would be more effective. Softening his tone, he explained to his would-be-gunner, "For now, I need you to find a way to turn on the protector field. Firing the guns can come later."

"As you say," Kalgun-dev reluctantly agreed and move to perch on the high-backed stool at the gunner's position. He fidgeted on his newfound seat as he peered through the translator device at the console in front of him. "This may take some time," he commented.

"As long as it is done before they fire on us, it will be enough," Leeyak-dar replied and stalked back to his place in the command cabin. Perching on his on seat, he sympathized with the raid-master.

CHAPTER 12

CSV Brookhaven
Sector 6, Alpha Centauri AB XII (Styx) orbit, 40 AU from primary
2215NOV13 00:48 CUT

"Captain, I've got something," Atticus announced as she made a further adjustment to her display. With a final stab at the controls, she added, "On screen."

A bright new yellow marker popped up among the silver indicators that denoted the few asteroids and comets at this edge of the system. Slowly, text was added to the yellow blob to provide information on distance and probable mass.

"Is that our missing frigate?" Midthunder asked.

Atticus shrugged. "It has the right mass, but I'm not detecting any signals from it and it's not responding to IFF. But the really strange thing is – it's not drifting. It's under power and headed out of the system."

The lieutenant's head snapped to the side to focus on the chief petty officer at the ops station. "How?" he demanded, struggling for any of this to make sense.

Before Atticus could respond, Basco announced, "Report from Center. Beacon is operating within expected parameters. But there is a problem with *Alexander*. The ship's transponder is sending the period pulse, but the timestamps are incorrect. And it won't respond to any other commands. All other ship transponders are operating correctly and returning to correct positions. The only anomaly is the transponder for *Alexander*."

"Because it's not really there," Midthunder mumbled, wondering just what was communicating with the beacon at this moment. "Hail that unknown ship," he ordered, though he suspected the yellow marker was all too familiar to his ship and crew.

The crewman at comms complied but quickly shook his head. "No response on any channel," he informed his captain.

The lieutenant chewed on that information for only a second. "Send the command to shut down power on the transponder channel."

Basco nodded as he set to work but was soon shaking his head once more. "Still no response. I can't even be certain it's receiving our signals. No handshake at all."

Midthunder slapped the arm of his chair in frustration. "XO, pursuit course. Full speed."

"Pursuit course full speed, aye," Özdemir replied automatically as her hands tapped out instructions on the console. "They have a lead on us; range point-one AU. Intercept in eight minutes," she announced confidently. A moment later, that look faded as her hands flowed across the controls. "Correction, target is accelerating. New projection is to overtake in fourteen minutes." She turned in her seat and looked to the captain. "If that really is *Alexander* and she goes to full speed, we might not ever catch her. Not before she can engage her StarDrive."

LT Midthunder slumped back into his chair. The one thing that separated *Brookhaven* from the *Nottingham*-class corvettes it resembled was what was missing – his ship had no FTL drive. This was perfectly fine since her mission was to patrol the storage zone; apparently none of the designers back at Fleet command ever considered that a gunboat might have to chase one of the starships it was charged with protecting. *Well, someone certainly dropped the ball on that one*, he mused. With a weary exhale he ordered, "Maintain course and speed. We'll just have to hope those old engines aren't up to full specs." Looking over to the comms station, he continued, "Inform Center of our situation and provide all the sensor data we have. Let them know we have a runaway."

Shad-var Swift-Raider Dominator
GC 46712-BLUE-2, 40.5 AU from primary
1582:298:05:05:08 KT (2215NOV13 00:54 CUT)

"The *hooman* ship has changed direction. It pursues, Seventh," Choban-hath declared after speaking with the monitors at the rear of the control cabin.

Telrin-vak snapped in acknowledgement. He was pleased that the overseer did nothing to suggest that things would be different if he were prize-master inboard the captured *hooman* vessel. The male had been understandably upset by the Seventh's decision and readily gave voice to that anger, but at least had the wisdom to limit those remarks to the master's cabin. They both knew it would not do to have such dissent spread in front of the crew. Instead, they both focused on making this raid a success.

"What of the dark-skiff?" the master asked as he watched the icons move across the main screen. The green symbol that represented the Seventh's new prize was still some distance away, while the purple glyph that marked its pursuer was further still but growing closer. It would eventually catch up to the Seventh, but when? With luck, not before Elldor-min was able to spin up the prize's sphere drive.

Moving closer to Vak, the overseer answered, "It enters the hold now. Once the doors close, we can go to the Seventh's rescue."

Telrin-vak snorted. "No. That is not the plan, as you know. We will meet with our band-mates at the first feeding world. That is where they will expect us; that is where we will go."

Choban-hath lowered his voice but became more agitated. "Plans change. The original plan did not include a *hooman* ship chasing the Seventh from the system. We need to alter the plan now," he hissed.

Telrin-vak turned slowly to look at the younger male, orbits of experience in Vak's face halting the words that escaped from Hath's mouth and crest. "We succeed by adhering to the plan. Only when all is lost do we deviate. This is not the time to panic; this is the time to stand our ground and act reliably. We cannot call to the Seventh to seek his guidance, thus we must act as he has instructed," he responded with a cold edge.

The overseer swallowed hard before answering, "As you say, Master." He stepped back to signal he would say no more on the matter.

Telrin-vak moved forward and rested a hand on the shoulder of the female at the steering station. For some reason he did not recall the name of Naymur-elv's replacement at the post and he couldn't seek that name from Choban-hath after their last exchange. So, he avoided addressing her by name. "Steerer, prepare the sphere-drive. Once *Emerald Dagger* leaves the system, we will follow." For a moment, he had to keep a sneer from creeping to his lips. "After all, we are the faster ship. No matter what lead we give the new prize, *Dominator* will arrive first." Vak thought a little friendly competition between the two crews would serve the band.

"And if the *hoomans* catch *Dagger* before that?" Hath murmured just loud enough for the master to hear.

Telrin-vak rounded on his overseer, noticing the male's look was one less of concern than jest. Vak snorted. "Then our gunner will finally have something to do on this raid."

Shad-var Prizeship Emerald Dagger (nee CSS Alexander)
GC 46712-BLUE-2, 40.4 AU from primary
1582:298:05:07:04 KT (2215NOV13 01:02 CUT)

"Our shadow continues to gain," Naymur-elv reported as she studied the elements on her screen, comparing the *hooman* symbols to the translation on her device.

Leeyak-dar gripped the arm of his stool, crushing the padding as his claws punctured the faux leather that covered it. Where once he praised the ship he stole from the *hoomans*, he now cursed it as the shoddy product of an immature race. "Can you find no more speed?" he pleaded.

Naymur-elv ducked her head while keeping an eye on the screen. "Apologies, Seventh. *Dagger* has no more to give," she answered, knowing the answer was insufficient. Her first chance as prize-master, and failure continued to follow them.

But the commander had already moved on, turning his attention to the raid-master. "And the protector? What progress?"

Kalgun-dev threw up his hands and considered tossing the translator across the cabin. "It is as before. Only the front half of the ship is covered; the rear portion continues to refuse to come up." He pointed to the image on his screen: a schematic made up of unfamiliar alien symbols. But the two red flashing elements required no words to explain their meaning. "These connections must be replaced, but I do not know where they might be and I cannot ask the crafters to seek them out," the raid-master complained.

"No. They must complete their work on the sphere drive," the commander agreed. "Do we have guns?"

Kalgun-dev snapped. "The only working gun is at the front. We can do nothing unless we are willing to turn back and attack our shadow. And I doubt they are limited to a single gun and only half protection."

Mayvel-ahn chose that moment to pour salt into the wound. "Seventh, the *hoomans* continue to call to us."

"Ignore those calls," Leeyak-dar boomed. "They may have some way to gain control through the radio. Block their attempts!"

"Of course, Seventh," the crafter answered automatically before remembering her original issue. "The radio remains off. But without it, we cannot call to *Dominator* for help."

"Your master already knows what he should do. He has no need of more words to do what he must for Shad-var," Leeyak-dar proclaimed looking across the three in the control cabin. "What we need now is for our drive-master to do her part."

That was the perfect cue for Elldor-min to announce the success of her crafters, but alas, it was not meant to be. Instead, *garm-voshtee* passed until Kalgun-dev broke the silence. "Our shadow will be in gun range in moments," he announced solemnly.

Not one to miss a second chance, the drive-master's voice piped from their collar-radios. "The All-Provider has not turned away from us. The FTL drive has power!"

Ignoring the old female's superstitions, Leeyak-dar leapt at the good news. "Go!" he yelled at Naymur-elv.

The long-time steerer did not need further instruction. Her hands plucked at the controls on her console and on the main screen a silvery mist began to form, slowly at first but in moments it became a solid wall. With a look of confusion, she turned back to her commander to declare, "We are in under-space. I think."

Leeyak-dar was just as confused. Having never been inboard a *hooman* ship when it made the transition to under-space, he found the experience wholly underwhelming. Gone was the vibration of the sphere drive spinning faster and faster as the shell of the mini-verse formed around the ship. Missing was the jolt of thrust as that bubble-space separated from the true universe and the ship in the bubble began to move independently of the rest of reality. Instead, a curtain rose and then ... nothing. Dar doubted he would ever get used to this ship.

"Excellent. Well done," he sputtered as he looked around the equally surprised faces. "Well done to all." He tried to sit back on his stool, but his tail stump thudded into the back of the wretched chair. Leaping up, he ordered, "Set a path to the meeting place."

CSV Brookhaven
Sector 6, Alpha Centauri, 40.4 AU from primary
2215NOV13 01:05 CUT

"*Alexander* is coming into range," CPO Atticus announced. She left off the sentiment all of them were feeling at this point – *finally!*

"Target the engines," Midthunder ordered as he leaned back. He was looking forward to finding out just who or what caused the old frigate to suddenly bolt across the star system. After almost two years as *Brookhaven's* commanding officer, this was the strangest thing the lieutenant had ever seen, and he wanted an explanation.

"Sir? I don't think we're going to make it," Özdemir called out in alarm as a fog began to swirl around the frigate on the screen. Even though their ship lacked the technology, everyone on the bridge knew what was about to happen.

"Fire!" Midthunder called out in desperation, hoping to somehow prevent the quickly forming curtain from closing around his quarry. He knew it was a longshot, but at this point he had very little to lose.

Twin beams of man-made lightning stretched out in a valiant attempt to connect the gunboat to the escaped frigate. For a moment it looked like luck was with them and the pulse cannon fire would shatter the quickly closing veil of energy, but the beams passed by the frigate to port just before the sphere of light exploded in a brilliant flash and disappeared.

There was silence for a moment until Atticus spoke up. "Sorry, sir. The StarDrive threw off our target lock."

Midthunder slumped back in his chair, all of the pent-up energy of the past minutes washing away. "It was a gamble, Chief. Sometimes, you just don't have the cards," he conceded. He felt the tiredness returning. "Helm, plot a course back to our patrol route."

"Sir, incoming signal from *Huntington*. Commander Wallace asks if we require their assistance," Basco reported from the comms station.

Midthunder groaned inwardly. "No," he replied through gritted teeth. *This is all I need now*, he thought. *Wallace will never let me live this down. The captain who lost a frigate from the storage zone!* He shook his head. "No. Contact Styx Center; let them know that *Alexander* has jumped to drive-space. Provide the time and last known course," he ordered. Maybe someone at the base would be able to make use of that information. It might provide a clue about who just took the former Solar Fleet ship. He rose from his chair and turned towards the exit, saying, "XO, you have the conn."

"Captain, I have another ship on sensors. Bearing two-four-seven mark fourteen; range point-one-three AU," Atticus reported from ops.

Midthunder stopped mid-step as a surge of adrenaline coursed through him. "What is it? Who is it?" he demanded.

"Checking. There's a spike in energy," Atticus replied, reading from her screen. She looked up in frustration. "It's gone. Looks like it jumped to lightspeed," she commented.

Midthunder was not deterred. He peppered the chief with questions, "What was it? Did we get enough for an ID?" After a moment he asked in hushed tones, "Was it Feorae?" The lieutenant couldn't say what brought that last question to mind, but he wasn't about to second-guess his instincts now. He was in too deep.

CPO Atticus played at her console, tapping instructions, then swiping away the results from her screen. "No. No, not Feorae. It looks more … it looks more like it's Krayd. Small. Probably one of their caravels; an older model." She looked up and turned back to the captain. "That's the best I can do. Maybe one of the experts at Center can make more of these readings."

Midthunder was nodding the whole time the Roman non-com analyzed the data she collected. With a final, forceful nod of his head, he turned back to face Özdemir at the helm. "Ensign, set a course for Styx Center. Basco, get me Captain Bohamou," he added as he stepped back to retake his chair as he formulated just how to present what they knew to the commander of the storage zone. It would no doubt be an awkward conversation, but at least he wasn't going in empty handed now. "Now we have something to report," he said aloud, though the words were directed more to himself than to his crew.

Shad-var Prizeship Emerald Dagger (nee CSS Alexander)
Under-space
1582:298:06:10:12 KT (2215NOV13 02:37 CUT)

Despite the rocky start, Leeyak-dar was pleased by the extended stretch of calm as *Emerald Dagger* surged ahead, faster than light itself, to the gathering point. With one last glance at the large screen on the forward wall, the image like a flowing wall of liquid metal, he snapped his jaw. "Turn that off," he ordered with a wave of his hand and Naymur-elv obliged.

The prize-master knew she was in the minority in her favorable opinion of the majesty of mini-verse mechanics and how this miracle of alien design allowed ships to do the impossible – violate the laws of the universe. Elv understood the physics of the solution only marginally better than the average Krayd, but that still placed her in a select category among her kind. As she deactivated the main screen, she contented herself by moving the image to the smaller screen built into her console.

For his part, Leeyak-dar's initial elation at escaping their *hooman* pursuers and the seeming conclusion to a successful raid was quickly tempered with exhaustion. After nearly a full rotation sneaking into and out of the foreign star system, he was looking forward to a well-earned rest and a return to the more familiar stars of home. He looked down at Naymur-elv and asked, "How long until we meet up with *Dominator*?"

After consulting her screen and comparing it to the information on her data-plate, Elv looked up. "If these readings are correct, at least twenty rotations," she informed the commander with a look of concern. She knew the news would not be welcome.

"What?" Dar spit back as the steerer predicted. "The swift raider will be there in a third of the time. You must be mistaken," he admonished.

Naymur-elv remembered the words Telrin-vak shared with her before she left for this raid: do not back down from the Seventh if you know you are right. He will never learn to trust you if you do not trust your own judgement. Standing to give herself some measure of authority as prize-master, she replied, "We knew this ship was slower than our raider; the *hooman* systems are primitive. But this sphere drive is proving less capable than originally expected. It is at full power but provides only seven-ninths what was planned." With satisfaction, she waited to see if the old master's words would prove true.

Leeyak-dar eyed the young female for a moment, then wavered. "We must discuss this with the drive-master then," he offered as way of shifting the blame.

As luck would have it, at that moment the hatch opened, and Elldor-min stepped through. She was finally out of her air-suit and announced in a cheery voice, "Seventh, life systems are now on throughout the ship. The raiders can complete their work without need for those heavy suits."

"Yes. The gravity does seem too high," Dar commented. "And it's cold."

The old female shrugged. "Every time we adjust the settings, it only lasts for a *garm-maltee* or more before the life systems reset back to the *hooman* standard. We are still working on making the change permanent," she explained.

Leeyak-dar waved a hand in frustration. "We can deal with the weight and cold later. Right now, the issue is the sphere drive; it delays our meeting with *Dominator*. You must correct this first," he insisted.

The drive-master lowered her bony brow and shrugged in amusement. "The ship is old, even by *hooman* standards. It should be expected that the drive is less powerful than it was when first installed. That alone explains why they sent it to the trash pile. It probably should have been stripped for parts orbits ago. If we try to push the drive any further, it may fail. It may fail anyway if we don't push it," she countered. She saw the disappointment in the eyes of the Seventh, so she added, "We can try to see if there is any more we can do, but I make no promises."

Dar yielded. "Do what you can, at least until we are at Mid-port. After that ... it does not take great speed for *Dagger* to serve as a decoy. Or a trap." No matter the flaws in his new prize, the commander was determined to make the most of this ship, if only to justify the investment he already made in its acquisition.

"It will be as you say, Seventh," Min agreed. "On a softer nest, we have restored air and heat to the level below. There are cabins for the ship's commander and master where you can relax, as well as cabins for the rest of the prize crew. Indeed, there is much space since this ship is meant to have a crew far larger than that of our own sharp raiders," she informed them with pride. She gestured to the heavy male crafter that followed her into the cabin. "We will also remove those useless backs from your stools. Unfortunately, the ceiling is too high for grab-bars, but we can attach handholds to the consoles."

Leeyak-dar stretched his neck and shook his head while a bleating horn sounded from his crest. "Well done, drive-master. If we must spend more than two nine-marks in under-space, at least we can be comfortable. Once the feeding machines are working, the crew will feast. Well done," he declared, his eyes raking those assembled in the control cabin. "*Emerald Dagger* will serve Shad-var well, thanks to all of you."

CHAPTER 13

The Residence
Solaris, Luna, Sector 1
2215NOV13 20:15 CUT

FADM Erica Hudson straightened her jacket as the usher rapped on the mahogany door. Standing in the great hall with the panoply of flags clustered above them, the whole scene struck her as anachronistic, and she fought the urge to roll her eyes at the very idea of mansions and household staff. Still, her opinion was not about to change nearly two hundred years of tradition, and she understood it was just easier to play along.

Hudson didn't hear any response from behind the door, but the usher must have as he opened the door and stood aside to allow the admiral to pass. With the door closing behind her, she looked up to take in the view. Around her, the walls rose up two levels to a decorative coffered ceiling, with three of the walls completely covered by massive bookshelves; more books than she had seen since leaving Earth as a young ensign forty years ago. There was probably no place on the moon or Mars that held this many physical books. If the usher had been an anachronism, this room fit that same mold, appearing as if it had been copied from a historical period video. Only one man in the Commonwealth could justify such extravagance.

"Admiral, good evening. So good to see you again," the Regent declared as he rose from one of a pair of high-back leather chairs positioned to face the fourth wall, which consisted of a massive floor to ceiling window. Beyond, the sun was setting behind a copse of trees, their branches sporting just a scattering of orange and brown leaves.

Even though Hudson knew the windows were really a massive array of displays and the view was artificial, she could not help but be impressed. "Sir. I'm sorry to disturb," Erica apologized as she looked about the room, wondering if they were the only two here. "I tried contacting Miss Comparato but was told she was unavailable."

The Regent moved towards a globe that opened to reveal a selection of decanters and glassware. He selected two heavy crystal tumblers, splashing an ample amount of amber liquid into one while pouring a darker brown spirit over a collection of ice cubes in the other. "Yes, I gave Miranda the night off," he answered. He walked back to the chairs and placed the chilled beverage nearer to the second chair on the table that separated them, gesturing to Hudson to join him. "Bourbon on the rocks, if I'm not mistaken."

Hudson glanced down at her uniform and considered. It would be poor form to spurn the Regent's hospitality, she reasoned. "You're never mistaken, sir. And, after all, it is after five." She stepped over and lifted the glass, gesturing to her host. "To your health, sir," she toasted with a brief clink as the two crystal tumblers touched. Sipping from her glass, she took her seat beside the leader of the Commonwealth. "I must admit, I am surprised Miss Comparato isn't here," she mentioned in an off-hand manner. "Given the recent changes in the arrangements between the two of you, that is."

After sipping from his own glass, the Regent eyed Hudson for a moment. "Erica, I'm not comfortable being the subject of water cooler gossip around your offices on Terra Station. And I'm certain Miranda wouldn't like it," he offered in mild rebuke.

After four years, Hudson knew when the Regent was truly upset and when he was putting on a show to elicit a reaction. She chose not to give him that satisfaction and instead explained, "Sir, I meant no disrespect. Indeed, after all you have done for humanity, we all just want to see you happy. And well, we can all see that Miss Comparato makes you happy."

Uncharacteristically, the Regent blushed at that statement, drawing again from his tumbler in an effort to mask any facial expression. "Yes ... well," he began before pausing for a moment. "I appreciate your kind words. But for the moment, I would like to keep my private life ... private. If that meets with everyone's approval."

Hudson nodded appropriately. "Of course, sir. Not another word on the matter," she agreed.

The Regent took a pull from his glass and eyed his guest. "Well, we both know you didn't come down here to shoot the breeze. What's the issue, Fleet Admiral?" he asked with just a touch of concern.

Hudson placed her tumbler on the table and tried to recall the words she'd practiced on the shuttle flight down to Solaris. Unfortunately, all her preparations proved futile as she could not recall the words and instead stated flatly, "Sir, one of our ships was stolen."

The Regent stared at the head of his defense forces for a moment and then began to chuckle. "Oh, that's a good one. For a second there, I thought you were serious. I mean ... I actually thought you meant it. Stolen! Like that's possible." He had a wide grin on his face as he chuckled, but the grin began to fade as the Regent noticed that Hudson was not joining him in the levity. Finally, his face fell, and he asked, "You're serious, aren't you? You're really here to tell me someone stole one of our ships? How? How is that possible? What the hell was the crew doing at the time?"

"No crew," Hudson answered and, realizing how inadequate that response was, her practiced words returned to her. "That is, there was no crew on the ship. At the time. It's one of the old frigates we have stored in orbit over Styx. Part of the reserve fleet."

The Regent's head bobbed up and down as he took this information in. "So, we keep a bunch of old ships in some roped off harbor and now you're telling me someone just wandered off with one?"

"Well, it's not really a harbor in that sense," Hudson began but the Regent cut her off.

"Not the point, Admiral!" the Regent said sternly. "The point is, we leave a few dozen ships lying around and now somebody stole one. What happened? Did some idiot leave the keys in the ignition? How is this possible?"

The Regent's criticism was biting, and Hudson tried to rein in the discussion. "It's more complicated than that, sir. The systems onboard those ships are secured with a series of command codes and pass phrases to prevent anyone from simply commandeering a ship. It should have been impossible."

The Regent grimaced. "Well it wasn't. Obviously, someone left the keys lying around for anyone to take." He took a draw from his glass, then wagged an accusatory finger with the glass still in his hand, sloshing whiskey over the rim and onto the elaborate wooden parquet floor at his feet. "I want to know who is responsible for those keys. Someone screwed up here."

Hudson was shaking her head. "The codes are stored in the high security section of the Fleet's central command database, both here on Terra Station with a backup on Centauri Station. It can only be accessed by a handful of people – the base commander at Styx Center, the deputy chief of Fleet operations," she explained, then as an afterthought added, "and of course me."

The Regent grunted. "Well, I'm not going to fire you," he conceded, with the clear implication that others were not exempt.

"You're not going to fire anyone," Hudson corrected the leader of humanity. "Once we perform a thorough investigation of precisely what occurred, I will empanel a board of inquiry into the matter, and they will make their recommendations." From her tone, it was clear that Hudson would not allow any outside interference. "And if that isn't to your liking, well then, you will have to fire me."

For a moment, the Regent looked like he was ready to call the admiral's bluff, but at the last minute he surrendered. "Fine. We'll do it your way," he agreed and slumped back in his chair to nurse his drink. "So, what *do* we know right now?"

Hudson allowed herself a quick sigh of relief before diving into her report. "Every ship in the storage zone is programmed to transmit a periodic message to the center to provide status. Early this morning, the crew noticed a problem with the messages coming from one of the ships, the frigate *Alexander*. They asked the ship then on patrol duty to investigate. That ship found that *Alexander* was missing, and, in its place, a small transmitter was repeating earlier messages to disguise the fact." She sipped her bourbon, though at this moment she would have preferred water. "After scanning the system, they located *Alexander* outbound from the system. The gunboat gave chase, but the frigate managed to engage their StarDrive before she could be captured. Immediately after that, a second ship made the jump to lightspeed."

The Regent leaned forward. "What second ship?" he asked in surprise.

Hudson tried to tamp down her superior's concern. "The gunboat was able to get a partial scan. Preliminary analysis indicates it was a Krayd caravel. Not one we've encountered before, but a very close match."

The admiral's efforts came to naught as the Regent jumped up from his chair. "Well, that's just great. The Krayd were able to sneak into our backyard, the second most important star system after Sol, and steal a four-hundred-million credit starship right from under our noses."

Hudson tried to reassure the Regent. "I doubt *Alexander* was worth that much when she was brand new. Nearly two-hundred years later, she's probably worth less than ten-million in reclaimable materials to a scrapper."

The Regent shook his head. "Well, that's what the new one's cost. And again, Admiral, not the point." He began to pace. "The point is, the Krayd now have one of our ships ... one of our warships!"

"Sir, we strip those ships of anything critical before they go into storage. Weapons are disabled and the parts stored; the computer systems are wiped clean of any sensitive information. None of *Alexander's* access codes can be used against us. At most, they have the navigation database, but that's at least ten years out of date." She stood when the Regent continued to move about the room. "The Krayd will not be able to use *Alexander* against any of our ships. They won't be able to sneak into our star systems without being detected the moment they come out of drive-space."

The Regent stopped pacing and returned to his chair. "Not our systems; other systems. If that ship was taken by humans, Solar Fleet could handle it; we'd alert the Tyndal as well. But with the Krayd involved, that ship might be anywhere. And as far as the rest of the galaxy is concerned, that will be an Earth ship attacking them," he insisted. "They aren't going to bother checking the name on the side. We'll be responsible." He took a healthy gulp from his tumbler, draining the contents and setting the glass aside.

"Sir, other races have lost ships to the Krayd. We've lost ships before," Hudson offered in an attempt to reason with the prime executive of the Commonwealth.

"Not like this," he threw back. "We lost freighters before, not warships. And even then, they were single ships alone in deep space; not parked next to dozens of others, all under the supposedly watchful eye of our Fleet. Those other ships were just unlucky. This makes us look incompetent."

The Fleet Admiral took that like a slap in the face. "Sir, this was unprecedented. None of us anticipated a brazen act this deep into our territory. We expect these things around the outer colonies, not at the heart of the Commonwealth."

The Regent was shaking his head. "It doesn't matter, Erica. It's done. Now, I want that ship found, whatever it takes. This is a top priority. I don't care if you blow it up; I don't care if you sink it. Just get that frigate out of Krayd hands."

"Yes, sir," Hudson answered with a sigh. She polished off the rest of her drink, then stood with a casual, "If there's nothing else, sir."

The Regent stood as well and extended a hand. "Erica, I'm not blaming you. And despite my earlier comments, I'm not blaming anyone else. What's done is done. I just want us to fix it now. You understand," he offered.

Hudson took the proffered hand. "Of course, sir. We'll take care of it," she answered weakly. She moved to the exit, adding, "Good night, sir."

"Good night, Erica. And good luck," the leader of the Commonwealth replied as he watched her open the door and step back into the great hall.

Hudson waved off the usher who must have been waiting for her return and strolled across the hall to the main doors, glancing up at the flags that adorned the space. *That could have gone better. It also could have gone much worse*, she reasoned as she left the residence. Still, she had no idea how she was going to fulfill the promise she just made to the Regent. With only the sensor readings from the gunboat, they had no idea where the frigate was headed when it left Alpha Centauri. *Alexander* might be anywhere at the moment. *How am I going to find it?* she wondered.

Shad-var Swift-Raider Dominator
GC 46684-VIOLET-13, 7.5 AU from primary
1582:307:07:13:14 KT (2215NOV22 03:49 CUT)

Telrin-vak watched as the screen cleared and the blackness of space once more surrounded *Dominator*. After six rotations in under-space, the return to normal was welcome and he moved to address the steerer at her position. "Make a path to second world," he ordered.

They arrived in a small system, with only 2 minor worlds bracketing the Kray-da-like world that circled the weak star. The world was barely tolerable, but according to the information the Seventh purchased, there was a supply of game animals on the northern continent. Hopefully these would prove more edible than the beasts gathered from their last attempted hunt before *Emerald Dagger* was captured.

"As you say, Master," the new steerer acknowledged. "We arrive in four *garm-liktee*."

Four, Vak thought with chagrin. Because this was an unfamiliar system, Dominator returned from under-space well away from the star and its few worlds. There was no need for concern – *Emerald Dagger* would join them in another eleven rotations; the crew of *Dominator* had ample time to prepare for its arrival. He turned to Choban-hath, who stood behind him supervising the monitors. "Overseer, see that the lander is made ready. And inform our remaining raider that I expect fresh meat at the next feeding."

The overseer hurried to stand beside Vak, his head tilted to the side in a look of concern. In a hushed voice he asked, "Master? Are you certain? She is a female." This last he said as if revealing the raider to be an Ooverg slave.

Telrin-vak struggled to keep the gurgle of mirth from bubbling out. "I am aware of that, Overseer." He looked the male in the eye. "She was selected by our raid-master. Do you question his wisdom in placing her on this ship?"

Hath flexed his elbows. "The raid-master also chose to leave her here rather than take her on the raid. But that is not my reason. I do not question her skill with a projectile thrower, or even her tracking skills for the hunt. She is alone; how can she carry the beasts back to the lander?"

Vak had to admit that the overseer made a valid point. "What do you suggest?" he asked.

Choban-hath said nothing, but his eyes flicked forward to the male at the weapons console.

Telrin-vak snapped his jaw in agreement before calling out, "Gunner, how are your skills with the projector rifle?"

The young male jumped when he was called, and announced proudly, "A gun is a gun, Master. I can kill as easily with a projector as with *Dominator's* guns."

Vak gurgled at the arrogance. "I will remind you of that when you return. You will go with the raider to hunt for us. Try not to disintegrate our food." He turned to Choban-hath, "Control is yours, Overseer. I go to my cabin to rest."

Hath bobbed his head and after a short whistle of acknowledgement, he confessed, "As you say, Master. But I am uneasy. More than a nine-mark in this place. What if we are discovered?"

Telrin-vak snapped his jaw. "At worst, another band might stop here to forage. You must relax, Hath. We escaped the *hoomans*. The hard part is behind us now."

THE SERPENT'S TOOTH

Shad-var Prizeship Emerald Dagger (nee CSS Alexander)
Under-space, en route to GC 46684-VIOLET-13
1582:310:11:04:04 KT (2215NOV25 08:19 CUT)

Dar was relaxing in his cabin when he felt it the first time. His stomachs were still bothering him after another unsatisfactory first feeding. While the crafters were able to turn on the *hooman* feeding machines, there was little they could do to control what the devices produced. Though the *hooman* slaves the band held ate whatever nourishment their keepers provided, on their own ships they were masters, and their choices confounded the Krayd.

Most of the meals the machines provided included cooked meat, in many cases charred and burnt beyond recognition. Each attempt by the crafters to correct this situation failed; one even theorized that the machine was unable to produce raw meat – that the evil device actually created the meat already cooked, as if that were even possible.

There were only one or two items the machine would produce in raw form. One was a form of raw fish wrapped in rice; the other was another form of raw fish, this time in a slimy red sauce. Neither was appealing, but Dar found that if he stripped away the worthless rice, he was able to choke down the fish without gagging ... too much. Unsurprisingly, the food was also lacking in several key elements the Krayd body required, so they were forced to make use of the packaged food at every other feeding. The Seventh chose to consume his nauseating meal at the early feeding rather than the last feeding, fearing that if he slept with that noxious substance in his belly, he was more likely to soil his nest.

Not that the nest in his cabin would have suffered in any way from such an occurrence. Apparently, *hoomans* rested on a hard shelf with only a thin layer of padding and with no source of heat to protect the user from the chill air of their ships. Dar found the whole thing barbaric and wondered how these creatures ever managed electricity much less the ability to travel the stars.

The cabin shook again, more violently than the first time and in a blink Naymur-elv's voice called down from the ceiling above him. "Seventh, you are needed in the control cabin," the prize-master advised him.

Luckily, Leeyak-dar was already dressed since there was nothing that would induce him to strip away his leathers – no nice warm nest and the bathing facilities on the ship were inadequate at best and verging on criminal at worst. He wasted no time scrambling through the connectway and climbing the upway to the control cabin. Once there, he demanded, "What is happening?"

Naymur-elv, standing over her console, gripping the recently installed rail, answered, "It is the drive, Seventh. According to the drive-master, the two …," she paused looking for the proper term before tossing out, "pods are out of sync. She noticed it last rotation and assumed the system would correct itself, but it is getting worse."

"Stupid *hooman* design," Dar muttered. "What can be done?"

The prize-master bowed her head. "We must shut down. The drive-master can do nothing while the system is operating."

"Shut down where, Prize-master? In the middle of the void?" the Seventh challenged. He snapped his jaw and waved an arm, forestalling any reply to his question. "Very well. Steer for the closest star system. We will call *Dominator* to join us there."

"Seventh," Mayvel-ahn spoke up in alarm. "The radio … there is no star-caller!"

"What?" Dar exploded. "That is impossible. I have seen the documents. They call it," he bellowed, then stumbled over the alien term, "high-period."

"Hyperion," Ahn corrected her superior, then immediately regretted doing so. She plunged forward with her explanation in the hopes that the Seventh did not notice her gaff. "It is a faster-than-light signal, but it is only designed for short distances. Less than forty-five *zel-hosh*."

Leeyak-dar fumed. "Impossible! What kind of idiot would design a starship without the ability to radio to its home system for aid?"

"A *hooman* idiot," Naymur-elv offered. She wanted to redirect the Seventh's wrath away from the young crafter.

And she succeeded as Leeyak-dar angrily spun towards her. "Do you have anything useful to say, prize-master?"

Elv lifted her head high. "We must reach a system where we can radio for *Dominator*. But there is nothing marked along our path. Not unless there is some hidden cache of supplies still available at the old far-port," she declared bravely, ready to defend her assessment of the situation if necessary. She was prize-master, after all, and it was time she acted like one.

Leeyak-dar seethed, ready to slash out at his jacked-up steerer at first. *Did this child just deliberately bring up the source of my past failure? I should gut her for such impudence!* he raged silently. But the fury ebbed as a memory jumped up to replace it. "No," he replied through bared teeth, the tones from his crest lingering as he regained control. "No," he repeated and grabbed for the data-plate in the pouch that dangled from his belt. Pulling the device out, he stabbed at the controls furiously until, at last, he found the information he sought. Thrusting the device at Naymur-elv, he answered. "Not the old far-port. But here!"

Naymur-elv stared at the information for a moment. "Four-six-seven-oh-seven-YELLOW-eight," she read off, then leaned over and entered the designation into the navigation system. On her small screen, the ship's projected path was marked out as a dotted blue line. From that, a brief yellow branch broke off until it reached a nearby star system. "Why there, Seventh? Is there a secret Shad-var base in this system?"

"No. Not a Shad-var base," Leeyak-dar admitted. "Rotations ago, when we first built the far-port, other bands sought to beat us to the prize. One tried to create their own base in this system. As far as I know, it was never completed. But there might still be supplies there that we can use."

"And a radio?" Elv asked as she stood up.

A chortle escaped the Seventh's crest. "I have heard the Proh-zog called many things, but never has anyone called them stupid," he advised. "There will be a radio there; there may be other useful items."

The prize-master was still skeptical. "This system can be reached, but it will take at least two *garm-liktee*. Assuming the drive holds that long."

As if on cue, a shudder ran through the deck; less than the last, but still noticeable. Dar snapped his jaw and stretched out his neck. "You will do what must be done, Prize-master. Of that I have no doubt." With a final glance around the cabin, he turned and exited.

Naymur-elv bent over her console and made the necessary adjustments to their course. As she did so, she wondered if even the Seventh believed the words he just spoke.

CHAPTER 14

Shad-var Prizeship Emerald Dagger (nee CSS Alexander)
Under-space, en route to GC 46707-YELLOW-8
1582:310:13:11:09 KT (2215NOV25 11:31 CUT)

All eyes in the control cabin were fixed on the main screen as Naymur-elv counted up to their return to real space, "… six, seven, eight … return!" The rippling wall of silver exploded in a flash of light, but unlike any experience any of them had before, the ship's gravity shifted dramatically as if the ship had struck something. The group pitched forward, and the crew was lucky to have the handholds installed earlier by the crafters.

"What was that?" Leeyak-dar cried out as he steadied himself. Once the artificial gravity settled, he examined his hand to find a ragged line across his palm and white blood already oozing from the gash. His tongue flicked out and he tasted the scent of blood in the air; he was not the only one injured.

The prize-master pushed herself up from the console with blood dripping down on her vest from the cut on her jaw where she struck the controls in front of her. It took a moment for her to catch her breath before she could answer. "The drive," she choked out and she studied the symbols on her screen. After tapping a few controls, she explained, "The strain of return caused a final surge. The bubble did not collapse correctly. Possibly because the ship was not centered in the field."

Dar bobbed his head, though in truth he only understood half of the explanation Naymur-elv provided. Perhaps less than half if he was being honest. But the important part was that they had survived, so he tried to present a confident front. "Take us to the first world," he instructed.

Elv set to work, but her reaction after pressing a few controls revealed concern. "The near-space drive is sluggish; it is possible it was damaged during the return."

Dar leaned forward on his stool as he flexed his damaged hand. "Will we be able to reach the world?" he asked, not bothering to hide the concern in his voices.

"I believe so, but it will take the rest of the rotation," the prize-master answered after checking her console. "Assuming the near-space drive does not get any worse."

Leeyak-dar looked about. A few rotations ago, *Dagger* was the shining symbol of his return to power. Now he wondered if the prizeship would ever leave this system. The sudden change in fortune was nearly too much to bear. "Speak to the drive-master; tell her to do all she can. We must reach that world if we are to contact *Dominator*," he responded idly as he moved away from the helm and towards the caller console.

Mayvel-ahn saw the commander coming and looked up in trepidation. "Seventh?" she asked weakly, a rising dread that the male would demand some action of her that violated the laws of physics. She kept her eyes down in the unlikely hope that Dar might walk past her at the last moment.

"Crafter," he began ominously as he towered above her, lifting a wounded hand to point at the console. "Have you mastered this device yet? I must know our options."

Ahn breathed a sigh of relief, and she bobbed her head and whistled in the affirmative. "I can operate it, Seventh. It is not too unlike the radios of other prizes I have been on."

"Really?" the commander replied with a touch of surprise. "I was not aware you were so accomplished. What ships have you taken before this one?"

Mayvel-ahn's eyes went wide as she backtracked her prior statement. "I ... I do not ... I did not raid any ships before. I was brought inboard after the capture to study the systems and provide instruction on their operation," she stammered. "A Travaillian scout vessel and a Feorae hauler," she specified as the Seventh's eyes seemed to burn down on her.

Dar's tongue flicked twice as he took this in, finally saying, "Good. Then you can work this radio. I need a message sent to the world we approach." He turned to look at the main screen, where the ship's path was laid out over a schematic of the system. At the moment, their progress was miniscule. "The Proh-zog are not an incompetent band; they will notice our arrival, perhaps even now. If we seek use of their base, we must show them deference."

"They will aid us?" Ahn asked in surprise. Most of her life was spent in Shad-var's isolated communities on Trogok; she had little contact with members of other bands and was taught at an early age to distrust outsiders and keep to her own kind.

Leeyak-dar chortled. "They will aid us. For a price," he reassured the female. "That is always the way."

Mayvel-ahn bobbed her head to show she understood, while in truth she did not. But if the Seventh said it was so, it must be so and it was best not to question. But a concern did come to mind. "Seventh, I can call to the world with the *hooman* system, but it cannot provide the proper encoding or cypher," she warned. "And I can only do that manually for Shad-var. Will the Proh-zog be able to read your message?"

Dar shrugged. "I will provide the coding, as I will decode the response they send back. You need only send the message I give you," he reassured the crafter, tapping a spot on the console.

Stepping back, he called out in a loud voice, "I am going to my cabin; I will not be disturbed unless it is an emergency." As he reached the hatch, he added, "And someone tell the drive-master to turn up the heat!"

Shad-var Prizeship Emerald Dagger (nee CSS Alexander)
GC 46707-YELLOW-8-1 orbit
1582:311:02:09:12 KT (2215NOV25 20:42 CUT)

Well past mid-dark, *Emerald Dagger* moved into orbit of the gas giant that dominated this system. After several course adjustments, they moved in to circle the small moon that the Seventh identified as home to the Proh-zog far-port. So far, there had been no response to the many messages Mayvel-ahn transmitted. To Dar, that silence was ominous.

The ship was considerably larger than *Dominator* and they found a dedicated meeting cabin one level down from the control cabin. The Seventh gathered his senior crew, while a raider stood watch in the control cabin, with clear instructions to alert the group if there was any change, either from the radio or from the various detectors mapping the surface below.

"Are we certain there is a base on this moon?" Naymur-elv asked as the group stood around the table in the center of the room. None of the stools in this cabin were modified for the Krayd physique and no one wanted to perch on the edge of the spindly chairs. She noticed the look the Seventh was giving her and added, "Maybe they surveyed the surface and changed their plans."

"Or we have the wrong moon. There are four others large enough to be suitable for habitats," Elldor-min offered. Unlike the prize-master, she ignored the glare from the commander.

Leeyak-dar did his best to hide the anger in his voices. "There is no mistake; the information comes from a most reliable source. This is the moon where the Proh-zog crews constructed their port," he insisted. He looked about the table to see if any would challenge his assertion.

The raid-master was the first to speak. "When we find this port, how will we reach it?" he asked plainly. The eyes of the cabin shifted to him. "We abandoned the dark-skiff and left the lander with *Dominator*."

Leeyak-dar dismissed the concern with a wave of his bandaged hand. "There are *hooman* landers; we will use those."

"Behind the cargo doors that would not open," Kalgun-dev reminded him. "And who will steer these alien landers? I have never done so, and neither have any of my raiders."

The Seventh had no answers for these problems, but luckily others spoke up. "I will work on the doors," Mayvel-ahn offered.

"We need all the crafters to repair the broken drive," Dev countered.

Elldor-min snorted. "No. She would only slow us down," she said with a soft eye towards the younger female. "Your skills are elsewhere. Leave the caller for a time and see to the cargo doors."

"I can steer the lander," the prize-master admitted; a tone of resignation from her crest. "If the controls are anything like the ship's, it should not prove difficult."

Leeyak-dar extended his throat and shook his head. "There! The issue is resolved. We move forward now," he declared. He wanted to end this debate; it was unseemly! This meeting should have been him giving orders to the crew, laying out **his** plan. *How did it devolve to this?* he wondered. Dar vowed that no record of this meeting would survive the journey. He could not afford to have anything taint his victorious return with *Emerald Dagger*.

Dar turned toward the hatch when the young crafter spoke timidly. "There is another matter, Seventh."

With a bleat of exasperation, he demanded, "What?"

If possible, Mayvel-ahn's voices grew smaller. "The caller. When I turned it on to send your message to the Proh-zog, something else was also sent." She looked about to find Elldor-min's face and continued speaking to her. "I did not see it at the time. But I was looking through the records, trying to find out why the port did not answer, and I found this instead. I cannot be sure, but I think the ship sent out a call of help."

Leeyak-dar was confused and his stance showed it as he demanded, "How?"

Stepping in, Elldor-min explained, "It is likely automatic. From what we have found, the *hoomans* rely on their machines to act without instruction in many cases."

"Then they are fools," the commander replied. The idea was foreign to Dar. How could you be in command of a ship if you turned over control to the machines? It defied logic.

The drive-master flexed. "No doubt; they are alien and therefore unpredictable. It is possible that when the FTL drive failed, the computer composed a message to send to their port. When Ahn restored power, the message was sent."

"Incredible," the Seventh commented in disbelief. "But of no matter."

Now Mayvel-ahn was confused. "No matter? It does not anger you that the ship betrays us?"

A gurgle rose in Dar throat. "No. You said yourself, there is no star-caller. That message cannot reach beyond this system. There is no one to hear it but the Proh-zog, and they are obviously ignoring it along with the message I gave you." He turned and headed for the hatch. "The ship can shout into the void until we return to Kray-da for all I care. It will be twenty-nine orbits before any of it reaches the *hoomans!*"

Terra Station
Sector 1, Sol, Terra orbit
2215NOV27 12:19 CUT

Erica Hudson was seated at her desk, staring at the desk display but not really reading the information on the screen. That had been happening a lot the past three days; she was unable to focus on things as her mind wandered. *Perhaps I need a vacation*, she thought but immediately dismissed the idea. There was too much happening right now to simply walk away for a week or two. *There is always too much and that will never change*, she admitted.

The sound of the door opening caused her to look up and she saw her adjutant WCDR Balakrishnan stride into the office, tablet in hand. The wing commander's bright red Solar Flight uniform was in sharp contrast to the dark ocean blue color of the fleet admiral's own. With a sigh Hudson asked, "What is it, Mirza?"

Balakrishnan fell into one of the chairs on the opposite side of the desk, placing her tablet face down on one of the few empty spots on the desk. Hudson had a habit of leaving devices and reports all over her desk long after reviewing them, and Mirza made a note of which device was hers. "The latest update from Second Fleet HQ. I forwarded it to you along with my summary."

Hudson leaned back in her chair and rubbed her eyes. "Why don't you save me a lot of reading and tell me what I need to know."

Balakrishnan suppressed a grin. It wasn't unusual for her boss to ask for a summary of the summary. Anything to try to keep up with the avalanche of information that came across her desk every day. "The ships they sent out to Gliese 412 and Stein 2051 returned to base. No sign of *Alexander* in either system. In fact, no sign of any Krayd activity. They're still waiting for *Tiberius* to return from Eta Cassiopeia."

The fleet admiral nodded as she ticked off the named star systems from the list she kept in her head. "Well, it was worth a try. It's been two weeks; *Alexander* is probably well beyond our borders by now." Hudson suddenly stood up. "I need coffee," she announced as she maneuvered to the beverage dispenser in the corner. "You?"

Mirza glanced at the two half-full mugs already on the desktop; the remaining contents no doubt chilled to the bone after a long morning. "Nothing for me, thank you Ma'am," she replied as she gathered the mugs and carried them over to deposit them in the cycler. She heard the machine flush the contents and flash clean the containers before dropping them into the queue for future use. She hurried back to her seat just as the admiral was retaking her own.

Hudson took a tentative sip of the dark black liquid in her mug even as steam wafted up from the surface. With a satisfying swallow, she took on a more relaxed posture. "We're not going to find that ship in any of our systems, or in any of the unclaimed systems nearby. We have to start looking further afield."

Mirza smiled. "An excellent idea, ma'am. But where?" Retrieving her tablet, she tapped out commands on the screen and was rewarded with an extensive list of stars beyond the nominal twenty-lightyear limit that defined 'Commonwealth space' in the minds of most Fleet officers. Even after she refined this to focus only on that section that led to Krayd space, there were more stars listed than there were inside the imagined Commonwealth sphere. "In two weeks, the frigate could now be fifty lightyears from Alpha Centauri.

We don't have enough ships in the Fleet to cover all of these," she pointed out.

Hudson sipped from her mug as she considered this. "We're complicating this too much. Instead of searching everywhere they might be, let's start where we know they have been," she offered. "Tortuga."

Balakrishnan almost burst out in laughter. "You want to check out the system where we destroyed their base? Wouldn't that be one place we know they won't go, since we already know about it?"

Erica was shaking her head. "It's been three years. They could have rebuilt; if not the entire base, maybe just a small refueling and supply station. And they might think the system is safe since we already scratched it off of our list."

"I don't know, Admiral," Mirza began as she brought up information on the star system in question. The 19 Draconis system was nearly fifty lightyears from Sol, near the edge of *Alexander's* current range and as far as any Commonwealth ship had ever ventured. From reports, there was nothing of value there once the Fourth Fleet destroyed the old Feorin base the Krayd temporarily occupied. "It sounds a little crazy – trying to guess that they would go where we think they wouldn't go because we know they know that we know they wouldn't go there." She stopped and put down the tablet. "This is all too confusing. But what do I know; I was never in the Fleet," the Solar Flight officer complained.

Hudson chuckled at her assistant's comment. "Trust me, it makes sense in a convoluted way. Sigma Draconis is the closest base; what do we have there?"

A few taps and Balakrishnan answered, "The light cruiser *Nuevo Leon* is on station until the end of the year, along with two escorts."

Erica nodded. "Good; that's Zhang's ship. Have Fleet Ops draw up the orders: he is to investigate Tortuga for any sign of Krayd activity. Avoid contact with any Krayd in the area. But if *Alexander* is there, she is to be captured or destroyed. If not ..." She paused for a moment as she considered what she was ordering her people to do, then decided there was no other choice. "If not, continue on to nearby systems. That damned ship has to be somewhere in the area."

Balakrishnan looked up after making the appropriate notes on her device. "And the escorts, ma'am? Should they accompany *Nuevo Leon* on this … mission?" The way she said the last word made it clear she held little hope for success.

Hudson shook her head slowly. "No. No, keep them at Sigma Draconis. Just in case I'm completely wrong about this. We can't afford to strip the system of its protection."

CHAPTER 15

Shad-var Prizeship Emerald Dagger (nee CSS Alexander)
GC 46707-YELLOW-8-1-3 orbit
1582:313:10:09:16 KT (2215NOV28 07:17 CUT)

"The detectors can find no sign of life. No heat; no power," Naymur-elv explained again.

Leeyak-dar stared at the image on the large screen. As seen from above, a collection of boxy structures, each connected to its neighbor by thin tubes, was nestled into the shadow of one of the craters on the moon below. Yellow lines highlighted those sections of the structures that were obscured by darkness. "But this is clearly the port the Proh-zog band constructed," he insisted. "Even these poor *hooman* detectors can show that. Is it possible those other readings are in error?"

"No," the prize-master returned, then couched her answer. "But it is possible that the port runs at minimal power when there are no Proh-zog at the port and no ships in the area. This would reduce the risk of it being detected by any but the owners. They could leave it unattended until needed."

Dar was willing to grasp at that unlikely chance; it was enough to satisfy his plans. "You will take the lander to the port, and take that one with you," he ordered, a hand stretching out to indicate Mayvel-ahn. "Restore power and send our message to *Dominator*."

Kalgun-dev stepped forward. "I should go with them, Seventh. In case the Proh-zog left any traps for alien intruders."

Dar was quickly growing tired of the crews need to constantly amend his instructions. It was a right he afforded Telrin-vak after many orbits of service, but these whelps assumed the privilege after only a few nine-marks. There would be a reckoning when they returned to Kray-da, but for the moment he decided to tolerate the insolence. Anything to get *Emerald Dagger* back to the home world!

He waved a hand of dismissal. "Do what needs be done but summon *Dominator*! That is all I care about at the moment." He twisted about and stalked out of the chamber, presumably to the seclusion of his cabin once again.

The crew watched in silence as their leader stormed off, each thankful that he or she was not chastised for some perceived failing. The longer they remained stranded in this system, the more unpredictable the Seventh's reactions became. As the senior member, Elldor-min was the first to speak, "I guess I will take over here while the rest of you are away. Try not to be too long; our leader might decide to leave you behind."

The shuttle was smaller than others they were used to, and even with the original seats removed and proper benches mounted in their place, the interior was cramped. As Naymur-elv predicted, the controls were similar to those of the larger ship and so she had little difficulty maneuvering the craft out of the launch bay and away from the ship. Descending to the surface, she kept one eye on the warning indicator, just in case the Proh-zog port suddenly sprang into action and tried to shoot them down. It was unlikely given the readings on the structure's power levels, but then everything about this situation was unusual and it was simply good practice to be wary.

"Do you see a landing platform?" Kalgun-dev asked from the bench behind as he peered over Elv's shoulder. Unlike other landers they had used, this one had a transparent snout on which the computer projected additional information, so the only way to monitor their progress was to look forward rather than at a more conveniently placed screen. Again, *hoomans* seemed to go out of their way to make things harder than they needed to be.

Elv raised a claw to point out an item on the transparency. "There's the platform. But there is no chance the connector will fit the hatch on this lander."

A gurgle of laughter rose up from Dev. "Then it's a good thing I insisted on bringing your air-suits," he replied. They were each dressed in their environment gear, which only made it harder to move about in the cramped cabin. Donning their helmets would only make matters worse. "Land with the hatch away from the connector, just in case the port tries to mate up to us," he instructed.

"Of course! This isn't my first raid, Raid-master," Naymur-elv responded testily. Seeing the way Dev reacted, she guessed that getting under her scales was his plan all along, so she quickly changed the topic. "Do you really think the Proh-zog left traps behind?"

Kalgun-dev flexed his elbows as much as he was able in their current surroundings. "We'll see. And we'll see if the codes our leader provided work or just prove we are Shad-var interlopers looking to plunder their port. You'll know the answer if I blow up."

From the back, Mayvel-ahn spoke up. "Perhaps we should wait in the lander while you open the hatch," she proposed.

Dev laughed louder at this than before. "Very good, Crafter. You will make a fine commander someday. You already understand which of your crew are expendable."

This talk was wearing on Naymur-elv's nerves, and she snapped, "We all go down and we all go back! Is that understood?"

Dev recognized that he had pushed too far. "Yes, Prize-master," he answered in his best attempt at contrition.

Elv allowed a whistle of fatigue to play across her crests. Jabbing at the controls, she announced, "We're going in. Hold on."

Proh-zog Far-port
GC 46707-YELLOW-8-1-3
1582:313:14:04:15 KT (2215NOV28 12:14 CUT)

The connectway was dark, cold and deserted as the beams from their hand-lights played along the barren floors and walls. Just as every other connectway and upway had been since the Shad-var trio entered this foreign port. The detectors on *Emerald Dagger* were correct – the place was abandoned. The Seventh offered no comment to this confirmation when the prize-master informed him *garm-maltee* earlier. According to the drive-master, he just wandered back to his cabin.

Like many structures on their world, there was no signage on the walls as you would find in *hooman* structures. Members of the band would already be familiar with the peculiar layout the Proh-zog employed; strangers would require a guide, or they would be hopelessly lost.

As no guides were available, Naymur-elv and Mayvel-ahn relied on hand-detectors to determine just what was behind each hatch, waving their devices along the path and slowing their progress considerably. Kalgun-dev followed behind, blaster at the ready, though for what he did not say. The two females chose not to ask, since the most likely answer was that he was using them as triggers just in case their missing hosts left any traps behind. None were found on the outer hatch at the landing pad, but who knew what they might discover as they probed deeper into the facility.

"Are you certain we're going in the proper direction?" Naymur-elv asked for the fourth time.

Mayvel-ahn knew better than to snap at her superior, despite how much she may deserve it. "No matter the band, power is always processed at the lowest level. Because no one wants to live underneath the fusion furnace," she explained again.

"Makes sense to me," the raid-master commented from the rear, drawing a dirty look from the prize-master.

Further bickering was prevented when Mayvel-ahn noticed the indicators on her screen suddenly jump. "Hold!" she ordered (despite being the junior-most individual of the group) and waved her detector around the frame of the hatch to her right. As before, several indicators flickered on the screen. "There are power readings here. Small, but well above the levels we've seen in any other place." She studied the color-blocks to the left of the hatch. The top one was the red and almond of Proh-zog band, while the lower block was a pattern of four colors: magenta, yellow, crimson and turquoise. The crafter made a point of recording the pattern, adding it to the map of the port she was creating. She grasped the lever and yanked down hard, but the control would not budge. "Raid-master," she called out.

It took three attempts, but Kalgun-dev was finally able to work the stubborn lever and the hatch rolled clear. Beyond was the second largest room they found so far. Mayvel-ahn played her hand-light beam around the space, briefly illuminating the distant walls. When the beam finally settled on one section, she hurried into the room.

From the open hatch, the prize-master watch as the crafter attacked a console, poking and prodding the controls until the screen hanging above the console gently glowed to life. With a feeling of satisfaction, Elv asked, "Am I right? Did we find what you were looking for?"

"Yes, but ..." Ahn responded idly before her voice trailed off like an echo fading away. All at once, she spun around, playing the beam of her light across a far wall and revealing a pair of orange cannisters sitting in an alcove that looked like it was designed to hold many more. After a few mumbled words she slapped a control and the illumination faded from the screen.

"What's wrong?" Naymur-elv demanded. When the crafter did not immediately respond, she repeated her request. "What's the problem?"

In a dejected voice, Ahn answered, "There's no fuel. No hydrogen." She pointed to the alcove, continuing, "That whole cluster should be full; eighteen cannisters in total. But they only left two cannisters, and even those are empty."

The prize-master's head bobbed as if she understood the problem. "All right. We just have to find where they keep the extras. Where would they store those?"

"There!" Mayvel-ahn shouted as if to some incompetent underling. "You don't store extra hydrogen! Not when they can just collect it any time you want from the world we are circling."

Naymur-elv steeled herself from snapping back at the crafter. "Well then, we'll do that," she returned in calm voices, hoping her example would influence Ahn to do the same.

It was not to be. "How? I didn't see a collector-lander in the landing hall we passed earlier. Did you?" Before the prize-master could finally put the insufferable underling in her place, Mayvel-ahn dashed towards the alcove. "But we can get the hydrogen from *Dagger*. We have plenty in the reserve; more than enough," she babbled as she grasped the handle of one of the canisters and yanked hard in an attempt to move it. When that failed, she turned to Kalgun-dev. "Help me! We need to take these to the lander."

The raid-master shrugged and stepped forward to replace the crafter and grab hold of the container. After several attempts accompanied by several hearty grunts, the orange cylinder moved barely a hand's width. Kalgun-dev admitted defeat by turning to the prize-master and explaining, "You must return to *Dagger* and bring back Norshel-gat. Together, we should be able to move each of these to the lander."

Naymur-elv was not pleased at the sudden change in status from two who were nominally beneath her. She was prize-master, after all. "And just how do you suggest we will unload these cannisters with you two strong males left here at the port?" she asked bitterly.

Mayvel-ahn chimed in cheerfully, "There are zero-gravity carts on *Dagger*. The drive-master can show you where to find them." She turned and walked out of the room; after a quick look at each other, Elv and Dev followed.

"Where are you going?" the prize-master called out as the crafter continued along the connectway.

Without turning around, Ahn answered, "To the caller room, of course. Once we have power, I need to send that message."

Frustration was building in Naymur-elv's mind. "And where exactly is the caller room?"

Mayvel-ahn threw her arms wide. "How should I know? I didn't build this port!" she yelled back in frustration. "And you should let the drive-master know we need the hydrogen; she will need to fashion a connector from the *hooman* system to the cannisters." With her final instructions to the prize-master, Ahn turned a bend in the connectway and disappeared from view.

The two masters stood in stunned silence until Kalgun-dev broke the spell. "Do you remember when she was too afraid to speak in our presence. I miss those times," he remarked.

Naymur-elv thought she now understood what the Seventh was feeling. "Go with her! Make certain that her newfound confidence doesn't blow up in her snout." She turned and headed off in the opposite direction. "I must go be everyone's lander-driver," she added in disgust.

Draconis Outpost
Asgardia Colony, Freya, Sigma Draconis, Sector 17
2215DEC02 20:11 CUT

CDR Hekmat was left cooling her heels outside the base commander's office while she waited for his previous meeting to conclude. Glances at the yeoman seated at the desk beside the closed door drew only sympathetic responses. "It won't be much longer," the young petty officer offered weakly as he looked up from his work.

Derya Hekmat was nearly ready to storm off when the inner door opened and CAPT Akimoto finally emerged. "My apologies, Commander. Sometimes the governor just cannot stop talking. Please, come in," Akimoto offered as she stepped back from the entrance. Once Hekmat was inside, she instructed the yeoman, "No interruptions. Especially from the governor's office."

Hekmat took in the office in a quick sweep of her eyes. While she had never set foot in this particular space, it was typical of so many others she had seen in the course of her career. A spartan workspace with only a smattering of personal effects to distinguish it from thousands of others throughout the Commonwealth. There was a block print on the credenza behind the desk, plus a holo-cube at one corner of the desk itself, though no image was being projected at the moment.

"Would you like tea?" the captain asked as she walked past her guest towards a side table where an iron pot sat on a brazier; small ceramic cups completed the scene.

"No thank you, ma'am," Derya responded as she noted the teal low gravity jumpsuit uniform the diminutive Solar Base captain was wearing. A marked contrast with the more formal Fleet blue standard duty uniform that Hekmat had on; one she chose when summoned for this meeting more than an hour earlier. *So much for making a good impression*, she thought.

Akimoto returned to her desk with one of the small ceramic cups, silently gesturing to Hekmat as she took her seat. The commander followed her host's lead and accepted the chair across from the captain while also away from the holo-cube on the desk. This gave Derya a better vantage point to observe the Base officer.

"Commander, I received a message from the Ssenn two hours ago," Akimoto began without preamble. "It was a complaint. According to the Ssenn representative one of our ships is in a system we're not permitted to visit."

Hekmat returned a confused look. "Where exactly did this happen, Captain? I don't know of any Ssenn systems in this area." Her confusion turned to discomfort as she asked, "No offense, ma'am, but why did they contact you?

Akimoto grinned. "No offense taken, Commander. I had the same thought originally. But it turns out the system in question isn't claimed by the Ssenn. It's claimed by ..." She paused and picked up the tablet on the surface in front of her, reading, "the ... Greeyyaann." The captain paused again, wondering if she was pronouncing the name correctly, then decided it didn't matter in this instance. "Yes. The Greeyyaann. It seems these people recently made a claim to the Chi Draconis system. Which isn't a problem for us since we weren't looking at that particular star – we already have more than enough of our own closer to home."

"True," Hekmat agreed automatically. "But why are we getting all this from the Ssenn instead of these Greeyyaann directly. I mean, it looks like they are our new neighbors, as it were."

Akimoto sipped her tea before answering. "I don't know why every race out there feels the need to go to the Ssenn when they have a problem with us, and frankly, Commander, I don't care. This is just how things are. I'm not going to be the one to complain about this; I'll leave that to the Regent."

Another sip of tea and the captain continued. "Commander, I need you to take *Buenos Aires* to Chi Draconis; find whatever merchant ship is out there and move her along. If these are the new neighbors, I don't want any trouble in the first few months."

"Are we certain it is a merchant ship, Captain? Are we even certain it's one of ours?"

Akimoto glanced at the details on her tablet. "You're right, Commander. We don't know if it is a Terran ship. The data from the Greeyyaann was not that precise. We do know it isn't a Fleet ship; I checked, and your people don't have any ships out there except for *Nuevo Leon*, and she was still here when the Greeyyaann claimed to discover the intruder, so it can't be her."

Mention of CAPT Zhang's ship reminded Hekmat of a second, perhaps more serious problem. "Captain, if we go off on this wild-goose hunt, *Geronimo* will be the only Fleet ship left in port. Captain Zhang won't be very pleased with me if I leave the colony with so little protection."

Akimoto understood the younger woman's dilemma, faced with conflicting expectations from two senior officers of equal rank. It was a position she found herself in more than once over the span of her career. Still, from the base commander's position, the answer was obvious. "As sector commander, I have overall responsibility for the safety of Sigma Draconis and the surrounding area. Chi Draconis is two days out and two days back. At most you'll need two days to find and communicate with whatever merchant freighter triggered all this. We'll be fine here while you're away," she reassured her guest.

"Of course, ma'am. It's just ..." Hekmat tried yet again to give voice to her concerns but stopped when the older woman put up her hand.

"Commander, the decision is made." Akimoto pressed an icon on the tablet and a slight hum sounded. "Your orders are recorded, and receipt acknowledged by your ship." Recognizing the pained look on Hekmat's face she added, "If there are any ruffled feathers with your squadron commander about this, I will smooth over everything on his return."

Derya leaned back in the chair and acquiesced with a simple, "Yes, ma'am".

The captain rose up from her seat and extended a hand to the younger officer. "Good hunting, Commander Hekmat. I'll see you in six days. Dismissed."

Hekmat accepted the gesture and departed quickly with a mumbled, "Thank you, ma'am." Once she was away from Akimoto's office, she let out a noticeable exhale as she moved down the corridor. At the first intersection, she stepped to the side and tapped the band on her wrist. "Record for Commander Mayasawati: Joko, cancel all leaves. Get everyone back onboard. We have an assignment. I'll be there in twenty minutes to discuss." She pressed the SEND button, then continued on to the outpost's landing area.

CHAPTER 16

Proh-zog Far-port
GC 46707-YELLOW-8-1-3
1582:318:15:03:13 KT (2215DEC03 13:17 CUT)

It took two full rotations to resupply the fusion furnace with hydrogen from *Emerald Dagger*, and still the caller remained silent. Mayvel-ahn spent most of each rotation in the port working on the caller, with only short breaks to feed and recharge the air in her tanks. Given the limited fuel available to the furnace they could not waist any power for life systems, so the structures remained cold and dark.

It was well past mid-light when she approached the Seventh in the control cabin. "The caller is working as well as it can considering its condition. I suggest we send the message to *Dominator* before next feeding," she declared.

Leeyak-dar eyed the crafter suspiciously, unaccustomed to her recent presumption of higher station. She no longer deferred to him as she should, and his first thought was to remind the small female of her place in the band's hierarchy. But he needed her skills, so he was forced to tolerate her attitude ... for now. But that did not mean he could not question her wisdom. "What do you mean by 'its condition'? Will the caller work or not?"

Ahn was growing tired of explaining technical matters to the ignorant, and she growled. "It will send, but at reduced power. The furnace is capable of only half power, and the caller requires more than it can provide. To reach the swift raider should only take two *garm-liktee* normally, but for us it will take more than a rotation," she answered.

Dar stared at the crafter for a moment. "That makes no sense. How can the change be so great?"

Elldor-min stepped in, hoping to protect her crafter from the growing contempt in her voices. "It is the nature of under-space,

Seventh. Half power results in an eight-fold increase in time. This is unavoidable," she assured him.

Mollified by the drive-master's words, Dar shook his head in approval. "Very well. Send the message. There is no value in waiting for an improvement that will never come."

"Yes, Seventh," Min agreed before Ahn said something that might draw the commander's ire. "But to be clear, we were planned to meet with *Dominator* two *garm-liktee* from this time. Will the ship still be there when our message arrives?"

Leeyak-dar chuffed. Finally, here was something that he understood that his crafters did not. "Telrin-vak will be there, of that you can be certain. The old master and I have worked long together. He knows I will arrive as promised, just as I know he will be there until I arrive. Send you message, it will be received."

Shad-var Swift-Raider Dominator
GC 46684-VIOLET-13-2 orbit
1582:319:08:01:14 KT (2215DEC04 03:47 CUT)

The feeding cabin was mostly empty as Choban-hath stepped into the space looking for the ship's master. It took no skill to find the older male perched on a stool at a corner table.

Telrin-vak was enjoying the last of his meat as he peeled away a strip of flesh and examined it briefly before tossing it back into his mouth. To their credit, the raider and the gunner made a fine pair as they were able to bring the carcasses of several large beasts up from the surface. It made a welcome change from the packaged meals they would normally consume. Vak had to admit, he was not eager to leave this space just yet. *Perhaps I can convince the Seventh to rest awhile after his long journey*, he thought as he swallowed the succulent meat. Travel on the *hooman* ship could not have been either pleasant or relaxing.

"Master?" the overseer interrupted as he skittered to a stop next to the table.

Vak looked up in mild surprise. "Hath? Have you eaten? You must; grab a portion and pull up a stool," he suggested with a hand extended to the place opposite. "We must send down our hunters once more. The larder grows bare again."

Choban-hath had already eaten earlier, and food was not the reason for his visit. He tried again, "Master, they are late! The time passed at mid-dark; how much longer do we wait around here?"

Telrin-vak pulled off another strip and dangled it for a moment before tossing it into the air and snapping it up before it had time to hit the table. "We wait until the Seventh returns to us," he answered. "We wait, because that is what we were told to do."

The response failed to mollify the overseer's concerns. "What if the Seventh doesn't return? What if he was killed or even captured? What do we when another band arrives? Or when aliens arrive."

A low whistle played across Telrin-vak's crest and he lifted the food bowl to examine the remaining greyish-red block, a small pool of juices settled at the bottom of the curved metal dish. The food was good, and it was a shame to rush his meal, but he had responsibilities to tend. With a shrug he lifted the bowl to his mouth poured the contents down his gullet, swallowing hard.

With the meal finished, he replied. "And what if the Seventh arrives to find us gone? Because we ran off to Mid-port as you are suggesting. What will the band do to us then?" He let the question hang in the air.

Choban-hath stood silent, knowing there was no good answer to the question posed. After a pause he finally said, "We cannot wait here forever. We must send a message to Mid-port and ask for instructions at some point. How long do we delay?"

The master hopped off the stool and straightened his vest. "Ask me again next-mark. But if you must, at least wait until I have finished first-feeding."

Telrin-vak stepped through the hatch to find the control cabin a surprising scene of activity given the time. He found Choban-hath at the center of that activity and moved to join him. "It is mid-dark,

Overseer. Why am I called? What threat do we face?" He looked about the faces around him and a thought occurred. "Is the Seventh here?"

Hath offered a data-plate to his superior, explaining, "Not here. But *Emerald Dagger* sends a message. It is for you alone."

Vak took the device and flicked his tongue to the surface to unlock it. The screen came to life and blocks of text appeared. He read through to the end, then repeated the process wondering if he missed something. The scenario made no sense to the old master, but the instructions from the Seventh were clear.

He looked over the group around him until he found the steerer. "Take us from the world. We will spin the sphere drive as soon as we are clear. Prepare a path for four-six-seven-oh-seven-YELLOW-eight!"

"Yes, master," the female replied and jumped to return to her post.

"The rest of you, prepare the ship," Vak ordered in a loud voice and was pleased to the see the onlookers disperse, but grabbed the overseer's arm to prevent him from moving. Once they were alone, he lowered his head. "*Emerald Dagger* has failed; the sphere drive is unreliable."

Choban-hath bent his neck. "Then we go to rescue the prize-crew. It will be a hard loss for the Seventh."

"No," the master replied. "We are not going to rescue the crew. We are ordered to repair *Dagger* so that it can be taken to Kray-da." He saw the stunned look on the younger male and admitted, "Our opinion is not sought; the order is clear."

Dominator was climbing above the star system when the steerer looked up in alarm. "Master, a ship appears from under-space!"

Telrin-vak turned to Choban-hath, who hovered over the monitor. After a moment, the overseer announced, "A *hooman* ship. Much larger than *Dagger*."

"How?" Vak demanded. "How are they able to track us?" A minor species, the *hoomans* should not have been able to follow them from their star system after the Seventh took the prize-ship. It may have taken over a nine-mark, but somehow, they did the impossible. But it didn't matter, they were too late. "Steerer, is the sphere drive ready?"

"It is close," the steerer began, but one glance back at the master caused her to change her mind. "But we can be ready now if you say."

"Spin the drive!" Telrin-vak ordered. Moments later, he felt the familiar vibrations as the three globes that extended from the rear of the ship began to rotate faster and faster. At the same time, the stars that covered the forward screen began to fade from view as a blanket of white enclosed the ship.

A final jolt and the steerer announced, "We are in under-space."

The master realized he had been holding his breath and finally relaxed. "Good! I return to my cabin," he declared and left the cabin before anything else went wrong.

CSS Nuevo Leon
Gliese 685, 8.1 AU from primary
2215DEC04 20:21 CUT

The light cruiser *Nuevo Leon* emerged from drive-space at the edge of the minor system, a single M0V red dwarf attached to the 26 Draconis system. A meaningless system that had nothing to offer most races – two small rocks bracketed a barely Earth-like planet with too little gravity and too little oxygen. But CAPT Zhang had orders to check nearby systems, and this one qualified.

The chief petty officer at the sensor station was in the middle of his scans when a warning light flashed. Tapping a few controls, he brought up the information the computers found worthy of notice. "XO, we have a contact. Bearing one-niner-seven mark three; range two-point-one AU," he announced to the woman in the captain's seat.

LCDR Davtyan looked over. "What is it, Chief?" She was scheduled to be relieved at 20:00 but chose to stay on duty for another hour while the ship settled in and the crew started the first-level scans. Her goal was to have that complete by the time LT Pereira relieved her in forty minutes. "Let's see what you found. On screen."

The main display shimmered and a blurred image of something in the blackness of space took shape. Several attempts to clean up the image only improved it slightly. "What is that?" Davtyan asked as she squinted and leaned forward in her seat, as if that would improve the computer enhanced image.

"Not sure, ma'am. Computer gives a sixty-three percent chance that it's a Krayd ship, but it's hard to say more than that." As the sensor chief explained this, a ring of gold became visible at one end of the vaguely greenish blob, followed by a white ball that began to form around the object. A sudden flash of light, and the object disappeared.

"Whatever it was, it jumped to drive-space," the chief said, as if any star-farer would not already be familiar with the process. He turned in his chair to address Davtyan. "Ma'am, should we inform the captain?"

The XO shook her head slightly. "Chief, whatever that was, it wasn't *Alexander*. Our orders are clear: find our frigate and avoid contact with any Krayd. As it turns out, that particular Krayd ship just did our job for us."

"Ma'am?" the sensor operator offered as a challenge.

"Log the incident and continue with your scans. We need to find *Alexander*; everything else is secondary," she explained, and she jotted down a note on the tablet in her hands.

The CPO was not all that comfortable with the commander's interpretation of their orders, but there was little he could do. He made the necessary comments in the log and resumed his scan where he left off. "Maybe someone at base can figure out what it was," he mumbled to himself and moved on to the next section.

CSS Buenos Aires
Chi Draconis, 8.1 AU from primary
2215DEC05 23:45 CUT

It was nearly midnight when the Commonwealth destroyer returned to normal space. LCDR Mayasawati had the watch, and he noted their arrival without incident in the log. Following procedure, he ordered, "Begin scans," then rose from the command chair. Even with his relief due in fifteen minutes, he needed a coffee to stay awake.

ENS Baek looked up from her console at the comms station. "XO, I have a distress call!"

"What?" the commander exclaimed as all thoughts of fatigue magically washed away. He moved to stand over the young ensign seated at her console. "Do you have an ID?"

"It's incomplete. Probable interference," Baek answered as she adjusted the controls in front of her while focusing on the symbols on her display. After a minute, she proclaimed, "It's … it's *Alexander*!"

Mayasawati's surprise lasted less than five seconds as he reached over and punched a button. "Captain to the bridge. At once!" he said in his best command voice. *Protocol be damned, this is too big!* He looked over to the lieutenant seated at the helm, ordering, "Get me a fix on that ship!"

The XO bound across the bridge to the operations console, displacing the young technician who jumped out of the way just in time. He stabbed at controls, quickly reviewing the results on the display before repeating the process. At last satisfied, he tapped the ship-wide call. "All hands. Set condition red. Full power to shields; arm all weapons." His voice filtered out of speakers throughout the ship.

"Condition red, aye. Pulse cannons armed; point defense cannons active," PO1 Nawaz answered back from the weapons station. He tapped a button and hissed, "Torpedo room, answer the call!" He added something else under his breath in his native Farsi until a flashing blue light on his panel turned solid green. "Torpedoes loaded and ready," he finally declared.

The whoosh of the bridge doors opening was followed by the captain's voice. "Ready for what, Joko? Are we under attack?" CDR Hekmat moved to take her seat even as she was closing the front of her rumpled tunic.

"No, ma'am. We found *Alexander*," he announced with pride.

Hekmat blinked in surprise. "*Alexander*? How?"

Mayasawati offered a bright smile. "Probably by being the only ship in the Fleet that wasn't looking for her."

Hekmat was still questioning this when Baek interrupted. "Ma'am, I was able to clean up more of the distress call. It's automated; repeating on a cycle. Severe damage to the StarDrive. Seeking assistance from any Commonwealth vessel in the area."

Distress call, Derya mouthed towards her executive officer as he shrugged in response. *Sometimes it's better to be lucky than good*, the commanding officer guessed. She looked to LT Mbabazi at the helm, asking, "Do you have a fix on that ship yet?"

Misunderstanding the question, Baek chimed in, "Signal bearing zero-eight-seven mark three down, Captain."

Hekmat and Mbabazi exchanged a look of chagrin at the young officer's eagerness. "That's almost a direct course to the inner planet of this system. A type J5 gas giant," the lieutenant explained.

"Then that is your course, Miss Mbabazi. Best speed to the gas giant," the captain ordered.

Mbabazi nodded and tapped out the necessary instructions. On the display, a schematic of the Chi Draconis system appeared, with a blue reticule to denote Buenos Aires' position at the outer edge of the system on the left and a flashing purple mark over the large planet to the far right. A dotted blue line stretched out between the two. "Best speed, aye, ma'am. ETA seven hours, fourteen minutes."

Satisfied, Hekmat stood up and moved to the side of her chair. "Commander," she called out to the XO. "Maintain scans. There was a Krayd ship reported to be with *Alexander* when it was stolen. I don't want it or any other Krayd asset sneaking up on us while we're focused on the frigate." Stifling a yawn, she added, "You have the conn. I'm going to go get some coffee." Derya didn't look back as she exited the bridge.

"Aye, Captain," Mayasawati responded even as he held back his own yawn and his mouth began to water. With the shake of his head, he turned back to his console. *She could have offered to get one for me*, he thought and resumed the sensor sweep.

CHAPTER 17

Shad-var Prizeship Emerald Dagger (nee CSS Alexander)
GC 46707-YELLOW-8-1-3 orbit
1582:321:08:16:15 KT (2215DEC06 04:49 CUT)

Leeyak-dar was in a foul mood when he stormed into the control cabin. "What is so urgent that I am denied my feeding?" he demanded of the prize-master. After the lecture on under-space star-caller dynamics, he was certain that *Dominator* would not arrive while he was eating!

Naymur-elv decided to keep her focus on her screen as she answered, "Seventh, we are being scanned. A ship arrived and is now headed for first world."

Knowing that whoever this was, they were not their anticipated rescuers, Leeyak-dar anger turned to concern. "Can they see us?"

Now the prize-master turned. "I cannot say; it is possible the gas world is their destination, but ..."

"But what?" the Seventh prodded.

"But ... it makes much noise. Its detectors are active and sweeping everything. If it were Proh-zog, it would not do so," Elv admitted.

The Seventh had little desire to see *Emerald Dagger* caught in its current condition by another band; he was even less pleased to be discovered by some alien ship. "We must move. If they come for the gas world, they can have it. As long as we are not here when they arrive."

Naymur-elv was alarmed and offered her reasoning, "That could make us visible to their detectors, Seventh. If they are scanning, it may be an attempt to drive any ships from hiding."

Dar was not moved. "Hiding? There is nowhere to hide here if the gas world is their goal. And if they seek us, it is better to maintain distance than to wait for them to reach weapons distance." He looked to the main screen and demanded, "Show me!"

Reluctantly, Naymur-elv tapped the appropriate commands and the image she had been studying was projected for all to see. While the alien glyphs were meaningless to the Krayd, the flashing red symbol of the approaching ship was not. This was the threat, but it was still some distance from the gas world they circled.

And Leeyak-dar meant to keep it that way. "Recall the lander; the crafter's work is done here. We move to spin distance," he declared.

Now Kalgun-dev was alarmed. "The drive-master has not completed repairs. We cannot hope to reach *Dominator*; they will come to us. Here."

The commander snapped his jaw twice; he was growing tired of the attitude of his senior crew. "Did I ask your counsel, raid-master? Do not presume to give what is not demanded of you," he bellowed and was satisfied when the male knew better than to speak back. Although he was not required to do so, he offered his own reasoning. "Even a few *garm-voshtee* in under-space will place us well away from any pursuer. A much wiser use of *Emerald Dagger* than waiting to be tracked down like a *poondaz*!"

Kalgun-dev, bobbed his head and Naymur-elv answered, "It will be as you say, Seventh." Both set about implementing their commander's wishes.

Leeyak-dar continued to track the intruder on the screen, now confident that he was taking on the problem head on.

CSS Buenos Aires
Chi Draconis, 3.9 AU from primary
2215DEC06 05:14 CUT

After a hot shower and a fresh uniform, CDR Hekmat was feeling much better as she read through the known details on the Chi Draconis system. A binary pair separated by less than one AU, the gravitational forces of the paired stars resulted in massively eccentric orbits for the three planets in the system. It was as if Earth was replaced with a second, smaller sun which ended up destroying every planet nearer than the asteroid belt – no Mercury, Venus or Mars either. Just an extra sun in their place, with a surrounding belt of rubble left over from the destroyed worlds.

To Derya, it seemed wrong to have a mixed assortment of asteroids as the innermost planetary bodies; nothing else larger than a grain of sand. The gas and ice giants were minor copies of Saturn and Uranus, minus the interesting rings. A slightly larger version of rocky Mars between them hardly spiced up the neighborhood. It all added up to ... nothing. There was nothing about Chi Draconis that set it apart from a dozen other nearby stars. Hekmat could not fathom what made this place so valuable to the Greeyyaann, but then she knew nothing about the species in question. *Perhaps they like boring places no one else wants*, she supposed.

"Captain? We have movement," the technician at the ops console reported. The man was filling in for the XO at the moment.

Hekmat ordered Mayasawati to his cabin to get some rest five hours ago. He fought the suggestion at first, but when Derya made it an order he had no choice. He wasn't allowed back on the bridge until 06:00.

"Is it *Alexander*?" the captain asked, certain that it had to be. *Unless the frigate's mysterious escort is finally showing its face.*

It took a moment for the crewman to confirm the captain's suspicion. "Yes, ma'am. It's still transmitting the distress call, and the source is in motion."

Hekmat looked to the helm. "Range?" she asked.

Mbabazi's response was automatic. "Two-point-six AU, ma'am. Time to intercept one hour, forty-eight minutes."

Too far, Hekmat sighed. "Calculate her course and speed; make adjustments to intercept at current speed."

The lieutenant tapped out instructions on the helm console, then studied the results on his display. "She's headed out of the system; adjusting course to zero-eight-three. It's too early to calculate her speed at this range. Will advise when available, ma'am."

Derya considered their options, but there was a concern nagging at the back of her mind and she needed someone to tell her she wasn't crazy. Punching a control on the arm of her chair, she called out. "Bridge to Exec."

It took only a moment for the man to respond, his voice drifting up from the speaker at the side of her chair. "Mayasawati here, Captain." There was no sign of drowsiness in his voice. If anything, the commander sounded eager.

"XO, I'm commuting your sentence. Meet me in the conference room in ten minutes," Hekmat ordered with a slight grin and wondered if that sentiment could be heard in her voice.

"Yes, ma'am. I'll be there!" Mayasawati answered with gusto and closed the channel. Hekmat raised a hand to her face as the grin grew wider.

With seconds to spare, the doors of the conference room parted and LCDR Mayasawati walked through at a brisk pace. The brush of short black hair that covered his head was still a little damp while the white tab with the silver fleur-de-lis on his uniform collar was askew. Hekmat wondered if she should have given the executive officer another five minutes to get ready.

Instead, she invited her second-in-command to join her at the conference table, pointing to a spot where a glass of dark brown liquid sat alongside a plate of fruit. "Tubruk, if I'm correct," she offered.

Mayasawati took the indicated chair and sipped the drink before him. A quick smile appeared, "Very good, ma'am. For a machine at least." He nodded to the heavy ceramic mug in front of her seat. "You do not wish to try it?"

Derya smiled. "I'll stick to the Colombian blend if it's all the same," she answered, then activated the large display mounted at the end of the table. The tactical plot from the bridge display appeared. "Things have progressed since you discovered *Alexander*. She's on the move and in all likelihood trying to escape us."

The XO studied the image for a moment, commenting, "At least she's not trying to engage us. It doesn't feel right going into combat with another Commonwealth ship."

"You know our orders, Joko – capture or destroy," the captain reminded him.

Mayasawati nodded slowly, spinning the glass of coffee in front of him. "But we are going to try to capture them first. Right, Captain?"

Hekmat was not comfortable with the question and let it pass. "You read the report. That frigate wasn't stolen by humans. It wasn't 'borrowed' by one of our friends. It was captured by the Krayd."

Joko shook his head. "We don't know that; it's just speculation. It might just as easily be some home-grown dissident faction," he countered. "The Krayd ship in the vicinity might have been helping them, or it might just be a coincidence."

"You think Terrans did this? How? And what kind of idiot is able to restart a StarDrive but not smart enough to turn off the damned distress call?" the captain demanded.

Mayasawati opened his mouth to speak but then closed it immediately. The captain wasn't wrong. The enclosed bubble FTL drive system the humans used was common practice among the starfaring races of the galaxy; whether you called it KolSon, Kavur, Alcubierre or warp drive, it all amounted to the same thing – isolate yourself from the rest of the universe so you could violate the universal laws of physics. Simple. Any race could figure that out, but they would have a lot more trouble recognizing standard practices and Fleet regulations unique to the Commonwealth. One was common science, and the other was the minutiae of human civilization.

"Alien idiots," he admitted.

The captain nodded. "Those aren't Terrans or Tyndal who stole *Alexander*. And it doesn't matter if they're Krayd or Feorae or some other group. They don't get to keep her!" She saw the disappointment in her second-in-command's eyes. "We'll try to capture her if we can. But if there is any chance of her getting away, we shoot to kill. Is that understood, XO?"

Mayasawati nodded slowly. "Understood, Captain," he agreed. After a sip of his coffee, he added, "There is one thing. It is possible that they know about the distress call; that they're doing it deliberately. They could be using it to lead us into a trap."

Derya drummed her fingers on the tabletop. "Yes. I had the same thought. So, we're just going to have to be careful out there, as we plunge headlong into a fight."

"Business as usual," the XO concurred.

A tone from the speaker interrupted the discussion and the captain tapped a control. "Hekmat here," she answered.

"Update on *Alexander*," the voice of the navigator erupted from the speaker. "She's only making half-speed. New time to intercept two hours, forty-nine minutes on bearing zero-seven-two mark one down."

Nodding, Derya replied, "Very good, Lieutenant. Maintain pursuit; we'll be up shortly." She closed the channel and looked to her XO. "Time to get back to work."

Mayasawati nodded and took a healthy gulp of his drink. "One more thing, ma'am. I don't suppose there was any kind of reward attached to being the person who found the missing frigate," he remarked with a suppressed smile.

Derya crossed her arms and leaned back. "No reward, Commander. But I can put you in for a medal. Something gawdy for your collection."

Joko looked pleased by the answer. "Sounds about right," he replied and popped a bit of fruit into his mouth.

Shad-var Prizeship Emerald Dagger (nee CSS Alexander)
GC 46707-YELLOW-8, ring 2
1582:321:10:15:06 KT (2215DEC06 07:22 CUT)

Leeyak-dar sat transfixed with his tongue flicking nervously as he watched their progress on the screen. Even unaccustomed to the *hooman* language, he had no difficulty understanding that the ship his prize-master assured him was aimed at the gas world had changed its mind. It was now racing to catch *Emerald Dagger*, and every dashed line and arrow indicated it would succeed. It was not a question of if but when.

"Can we not increase speed?" he asked once more.

The voice of Elldor-min answered from the other end of the ship. "The near-space drive is limited; we were forced to borrow parts from it to repair the sphere-drive," she reminded her commander. This was not the first time either and that fact was worrying to the old crafter.

Faced with no good choices, Dar smashed a clenched fist on the side of the improvised bench he was using. "And is the sphere-drive ready?" he demanded, his voices growing higher and louder.

"It ... improves," Min offered in way of an answer, not willing to get into the specifics of sphere-drive mechanics with the Seventh.

"Well improve if faster," Leeyak-dar shouted to end the discussion, then turned his wrath on Naymur-elv. "How? How can it track us? Our detectors are silenced, are they not?"

The prize-master accepted the implied criticism with grace. "Of course, Seventh. If they were reaching out, we would have a better picture of the ship that pursues us."

"Yes," Dar admitted. "Has that changed?"

Elv swiped a hand on her console to alter the image on her screen. "The machine still reports a seven-ninths value that the ship is *hooman*. One of its own kind."

Leeyak-dar waved a hand of dismissal. "The same as before. It still cannot tell us if the ship is larger or smaller than *Dagger*. If it carries more guns or fewer." He snapped his jaw in anger. "The machine is as useless as its creators!"

The hatch opened and Mayvel-ahn scurried into the control cabin.

Leeyak-dar glanced over to find the source of the noise. The small female had not returned to the cabin since they left first world and Dar spit out, "Crafter? No one summoned you. You should be with your kind, fixing the drives. Either will do at this point."

The confidence the young crafter demonstrated in the Proh-zog far-port was gone and her natural reticence returned. In timid voices she squeaked, "Seventh, it is ... I know ... how they."

"Spit it out!" the commander growled, quickly tiring of this distraction.

Ahn summoned all her courage and shouted, "The radio!" When all eyes turned to her, she continued. "That is how they track us; that is how they can see us at such distance. The message. The message the machine was sending. The call of help."

Leeyak-dar turned slowly, his brow down and his eyes glaring. His breath rasping. "You left the radio powered? You left that machine screaming into the darkness? You fool!" he shouted, the voices echoing in the confined space of the cabin.

If possible, Mayvel-ahn grew smaller. "But your said ... you said it didn't matter. You said no one would hear," she whimpered.

"Kill it! Kill it now before I kill you!" the Seventh screamed.

The crafter leapt to action, slapping controls and smashing buttons until the entire console turned dark. When that was done, she turned about, the fear still filling her eyes. She might have spoken, "I'm sorry," before dashing from the cabin.

Leeyak-dar sat on his bench, seething. Trying desperately to find a reason, some reason, not to hurl the whole sorry lot of them out of the air-chamber. *I am going to die because of the incompetence of my crew!* was all he could think.

CHAPTER 18

Shad-var Swift-Raider Dominator
GC 46707-YELLOW-8, ring 3
1582:321:10:16:16 KT (2215DEC06 07:29 CUT)

The swift raider returned to the universe and Telrin-vak lost no time setting his crew into action. "Silent detectors only; locate the gas world. And tell *Emerald Dagger* we are here!" he instructed.

Choban-hath worked the monitors in the cabin while the master stepped up to stand behind the steerer. Vak leaned forward to speak only with the steerer, "Take us sunward. Slowly. Until we have a map of this system."

The steerer whistled her understanding and on the screen the ship turned to face the distant yellow speck that was the primary star while its companion was too faint to spot. They knew this system had few planets and all were further in, as was the ring of small-worlds that shielded the twin stars.

"First world located; two and seven-ninths *zel-hosh* far. Path is provided," Hath reported from behind them. The steerer's hand rolled the ball under her hand and the image shifted with the primary now off in a corner of the screen.

"What of *Dagger*? Any answer?" the master asked again. Though they were distant, using the under-space radio would deliver their message in the blink of an eye. Given the text of the message that summoned them, the Seventh should have answered the moment he received the call.

The overseer snorted. "No reply yet. But detectors have found two ships moving away from first world."

"Two ships? Who?" Telrin-vak demanded.

Hath shrugged in response, "Unknown. We cannot tell unless we use scanners."

Vak hesitated for a moment but knew he had no other option. "Do it! Let's hope that they do not use our curiosity to track **us** down."

Choban-hath waved the command on to the monitors next to him. It was a while before he returned with an answer. "The ships are *hooman*. The smaller might be *Emerald Dagger*, but where did the larger come from?"

Where indeed? wondered Telrin-vak. *Did the* hoomans *track their stolen ship to this system? A side stop on the path to nowhere?* Before this-mark, he would have said it was impossible, but this was the second occurrence in two rotations. In two different star systems. Could the *hoomans* advance so far in just four orbits? It made no sense to the old master, but then, it didn't have to make sense. His orders were clear. "Steerer, adjust path. Go to chase speed," he commanded as he grasped the handhold above him. "Ready the guns."

CSS Buenos Aires
Chi Draconis, 7.0 AU from primary
2215DEC06 07:35 CUT

"Range?" Derya called out once more. She didn't need to; the information was printed on the main display for all to see, updated every few seconds. Still, it gave the captain something to do besides sit in her chair and stew.

"Zero-point-seven AU; weapons range in twenty-eight minutes," Mayasawati answered; as with the captain he needed something to do during the long chase and keeping her informed would do. A flashing indicator caught his eye, and he brought up a new image on his display. "Captain, we were just scanned," he reported.

"*Alexander*?"

The XO was shaking his head. "No, ma'am. New contact, bearing one-two-six mark one; range two-point-two-nine AU." A few more taps on the console completed the picture. "Ninety-one percent match for Krayd caravel, type C6. Designating Tango-One." He turned in his seat to face the captain. "She must be the energy surge we picked up before. It could have been a ship returning from drive-space."

CDR Hekmat didn't comment on the XO marking the Krayd ship as the primary target, a distinction that should have been used for the stolen frigate. Like everyone else on the bridge, Derya continued to refer to the Commonwealth ship by her name rather than as some nameless, faceless element in a training exercise. Perhaps some, like Joko, still held out hope that the ship might be saved.

"Is she targeting us?" the captain asked, and the idea that this chase was all part of some elaborate trap suddenly came back to the forefront.

Mayasawati returned to his display before answering, "Negative. At least, not a direct path. Present course has her intercepting *Alexander* … just before we reach weapons range. She's faster than us," he admitted with reluctance.

Hekmat looked at the main display as the newcomer was added to the plot, the dashed red line outlining the caravel's advantage. "Helm, can we increase speed?" Hekmat asked desperately.

Mbabazi was shaking his head subtly. "Sorry, ma'am. Mister Barclay's asking if we can reduce speed; we've been running flat out for over seven hours," he answered, clearly not comfortable being the bearer of bad news.

Hekmat wasn't about to argue with her chief engineer's concerns given their current situation. *Buenos Aires* would have no difficulty facing off against either of the two ships on the screen, but if they joined up that guarantee was lost. She needed some way of preventing that.

"What about a drone?" Nawaz asked from her station opposite the helm.

Hekmat looked to Mayasawati for any objection before she ordered, "Do it."

Nawaz tapped a control and ordered, "Prepare Hurricane," to whoever was on the receiving end. Moments later a green bar flashed across the top of the display: 'Hurricane-1 Ready'. The petty officer lost no time in reacting to that news. "Launching," she announced, and a new token appeared on the plot as the fighter drone sprang from its perch in the hangar bay and quickly began to outpace its mothership.

With satisfaction, Nawaz declared, "*Hurricane-1* away. Time to intercept: twenty-one minutes."

"Have it target her engines, Chief," Hekmat said with satisfaction as she leaned back. If the drone disabled *Alexander*, it would be much easier to deal with the caravel. And the wayward frigate would be stopped well short of the point where she could engage her StarDrive. One thing was certain – *Buenos Aires* wasn't going to let that ship escape. Not again.

Shad-var Prizeship Emerald Dagger (nee CSS Alexander)
GC 46707-YELLOW-8, ring 3
1582:321:11:06:10 KT (2215DEC06 08:03 CUT)

The ship shook briefly, and Kalgun-dev consulted his screen. "Another strike on the left drive pod. The protector field holds," he advised.

On the main screen, their tormentor danced and bobbed about, mostly avoiding the blue bolts of energy that flew its way from *Emerald Dagger*. Leeyak-dar smashed the bench once more as Kalgun-dev demonstrated over and over that he was a raider and not a trained gunner. "Can you hit anything?" the Seventh demanded.

The raid-master threw up his hands. "The side-guns track poorly; I cannot change that! And the pesky thing refuses to move to the front where I could use the main gun," he bellowed back, uncaring if such action offended the lofty commander at this point.

Leeyak-dar was watching all his well-laid plans crumble and it seemed there was nothing he could do. The prize that was going to restore his reputation was failing him at every turn. The only crew he could afford was inexperienced and ineffective, and that combination would soon prove deadly.

For several *garm-voshtee*, the small craft sent forth from the *hooman* ship harassed them. At first the thrusts had been random as if probing for weakness but now the little fighter's fire was focused on the giant drive pods that hung from *Emerald Dagger's* sides, while other shots targeted the vents of the near-space drive. And his prized ship appeared unable to stop the vile thing.

"It aims to cripple us," Dar fumed. "We must outrun it. Prepare the sphere-drive."

Naymur-elv looked down at her console, where a sea of flashing red blocks confronted her. While the color was meaningless to the Krayd, it did not take the prize-master long to learn that it held great importance to *hoomans*. She twisted back to confront her leader. "The drive-master has not finished her work. We cannot risk it again!"

Leeyak-dar growled. "And we cannot stay here. Even a handful of *garm-voshtee* in under-space will leave our pursuers far behind. Spin the drive if you want to live!"

Elv stood up quickly and turned on the Seventh. "No! The drive is not ready." She declared with her hands clenched at her side. "I am prize-master."

Leeyak-dar suddenly saw the problem clearly. He tried to order his crew to become better, but that was impossible. He needed to show them how things should be done! He jumped up and grabbed the smaller female, easily tossing her to the side. "You are nothing! I rule here!" he screamed, then leaned over the abandoned console.

To Leeyak-dar's credit, he was trained by the best Shad-var had to offer. He was taught at an early age that a commander worth his share had to be able to perform any function that was critical to his ship. During the long travel to this system and the interminable period when his crew struggled to repair the caller in the Proh-zog port, their commander focused on learning all he could of his new ship. While the others thought Dar was sulking in his cabin, he was instead studying the controls at *Dagger's* steerer and gunner consoles, pouring over the notes left by the *hooman* slave as well as those created by Naymur-elv and Kalgun-dev. If they were unable to follow his commands properly, he would do it himself. He would show his reluctant crew just how *Dagger* should be used!

"We will not lose *Emerald Dagger*! We will not become slaves to the *hoomans* because you are too timid," he ranted as he plucked at the controls under his hands. Before Kalgun-dev could free himself from the gunner's console, the Seventh stabbed at the final control.

On the main screen, the silvery mist began to form around the ship, slowly obscuring the little fighter from view. Crackles of energy played around the image, discoloring the wall as it formed.

Leeyak-dar was certain that he felt the old familiar vibrations as the spheres began to spin. "You will learn not to question me again," he declared as salvation enveloped him.

CSS Buenos Aires
Chi Draconis, 7.5 AU from primary
2215DEC06 08:03 CUT

The forward display was split with the tactical plot on the left while the right half showed the telemetry from *Hurricane-1*. The captain watched as the fighter drone danced about, avoiding any weapons fire from *Alexander's* point-defense cannons while scoring hit after hit on the frigate's shields. No doubt this was vexing to those Krayd that stole the ship, but so far it was having little effect on the old frigate's shields.

"She's not slowing," Hekmat observed dryly, her arms crossed again as she questioned her earlier enthusiasm for this plan.

"She's also not accelerating," Mayasawati offered from his station. "All we need is one lucky shot and her impulse drive is toast."

"Or we could ram her," Nawaz offered unasked.

The captain and the XO stared at each other for a second until they both said, "It might work." Hekmat smiled at the coincidence. "All right, Petty Officer. What are your thoughts?"

The weapons chief continued to watch the drone move about as she answered, "From the readings, the shields are weaker on the port side. A straight run in while firing the cannon to weaken the shield more, and then drive straight through the plasma vent."

"And hope you don't take out the reactor when you do that," the XO commented. "Because then there's nothing left to capture."

"Or salvage," Hekmat added. "That is the goal after all."

Namaz nodded but needed to point out the problems with this idea. "Of course, we only get one shot at this. If the shields hold, *Hurricane-1* will be destroyed, and we'll be out of luck. They'll be free to jump to drive-space."

The captain shook her head. "No one is stupid enough to engage that old StarDrive this close to a binary pair. They'll need to be at least nine AU out for that."

The executive officer looked up in alarm. "Uh, Captain. I'm not so sure. Look!" he exclaimed.

On the display the familiar process of a micro-verse forming around the frigate began as strings of energy stretched out to separate *Alexander* from the rest of reality. But something was off, and some of the strings formed only to change color and others broke and faded away. When the cocoon was still only partially formed, the blinding flash of light came, although this time it was a prismatic splash of the full spectrum of colors instead of the more familiar blue-white explosion they were all familiar with. The telemetry from *Hurricane-1* was lost the instant that flash touched it a thousand meters astern, and the drone was destroyed. The display automatically switched to the forward view from *Buenos Aires*.

"What was that?" Derya asked in surprise but before anyone answered, a second explosion appeared.

Mayasawati jumped on his console. "Captain, she's back. I think. Maybe," the executive officer mumbled as he rattled off information even as he was trying to understand the readings in front of him. "It's not good. I'm not sure, but I think … I think the bubble ruptured." Another few seconds and he advised. "Range three-point-seven gigameters."

A fraction of an astronomical unit. "Helm, reduce speed. Take us to one quarter," the captain ordered. With *Alexander* now stopped after her failed escape, the destroyer was quickly closing on her position.

"Ma'am, I have visual," Mayasawati declared and the image on the display was replaced. In the blackness of space, a web of glowing strands twisted and spun around each other like a jagged rip in the fabric of the universe. Some were fading while others continued to burn bright. Silence filled the bridge.

"Is that?" Hekmat started.

"*Alexander*," the XO confirmed. "From the analysis, scanners can account for most of her mass and elements. It goes on for at least eleven kilometers. It looks like the micro-verse collapsed almost immediately. The ship returned to real-space one particle at a time at lightspeed."

No spacer could imagine of a worse way to die – your atoms stretched out and scattered across the universe. Instant nothingness. Derya was thankful that she had not eaten for hours; it made it easier to hold down what little was there. "Complete your scans, XO. But take that off the screen."

"Of course, ma'am," he answered, and the tactical display returned to fill the display.

Hekmat pulled the tablet from its holder and tapped a control. "Record current time. Starship *Alexander* lost in Chi Draconis system, coordinates to follow. No survivors." She regretted that the old frigate would not be considered lost in the line of duty, but that possibility ended when the ship was sent to Styx. Stabbing the control once more, she looked to Mayasawati "What about the caravel?" she asked.

The XO brought up a second display to check those readings, then answered, "She's slowing."

CDR Hekmat nodded slowly. She never encountered a Krayd before this mission, but she could guess what that ship's commander was feeling at this moment.

Shad-var Swift-Raider Dominator
GC 46707-YELLOW-8, ring 3
1582:321:11:06:14 KT (2215DEC06 08:04 CUT)

Choban-hath stood with his snout agape as the information from *Dominator's* scanners played out across the main screen. *How is it possible?* he thought. *How could anything like this happen?* his mind screamed.

"Overseer," Telrin-vak prompted and when he received no reply he shouted, "Overseer!"

"Yes. Yes, Master," Hath stammered as his attention returned.

Vak wanted to growl but knew better than to do that in front of the crew. "Are they certain?" he repeated in calm voices as his grip on the handhold was the only outward betrayal of his thoughts.

The overseer bobbed. "Yes. Yes, that is ... that was *Emerald Dagger*," he answered. He glanced back to the monitors, who likewise bobbed in agreement. "Should we ... do we attack the *hooman* ship?"

Telrin-vak considered the question for a long moment as the eyes of the control cabin focused on him. With a snort of anger, he responded. "No! Take us away from here."

Choban-hath was stunned, thinking his original question so obvious. "But ... but ... they killed the Seventh!" he shrieked. "We must avenge him! All of them!"

The old master turned about to confront his overseer, wondering how he could ever have thought to promote this male. "I am the master here. Not you," he bellowed back. "Are we mammals? Are we Feorae who act out of some bizarre need for revenge?" he demanded. "We are Shad-var! We act for the band. How does attacking the *hoomans* profit Shad-var?"

Choban-hath stood silent, finally understanding his error.

Telrin-vak turned away from the male. "Leave the cabin; you have no work here." He waited for the sound of the hatch opening and closing before he addressed the remaining crew. "We are Shad-var; never forget that. I will send the message to the First; I will explain the loss of our prize." Looking down at the junior steerer, the faces of Naymur-elv and Elldor-min came unbidden to his mind. Their loss stung most of all, but there was nothing to be done now.

Resting a hand on the shoulder of the young female. "You have control while I am in my cabin. Prepare a path to Mid-port. We have no more business here."

EPILOGUE

Shad-var Tower, District 38
Ryok-dura, Oover-telz, Kray-da, Hosh
1582:331:08:01:05 KT (2216DEC16 03:16 CUT)

Orval-geeth came in early to scan the over-dark records and was pleased to have done so. The event she waited four long orbits to occur finally appeared after mid-dark. After reading the words, she wanted to celebrate but knew better. Instead, she maintained her normal routine, though the tips of her claws tingled each time she tapped a glyph on her data-plate.

She was engrossed in a record from Trogok on recent beryllium production when the portal opened and the First entered. She stood up quickly and assumed her normal attitude of service. "First, how can I assist?" she asked while lowering her snout.

Uncharacteristically, Sselmin-dor bared his teeth as his breathing grew raspy. "Why?" he managed to ask in low guttural tones. "Why was it necessary? Why was it done?"

The Eyes of the First took a slight step back from her desk as she calculated whether or not the principal might be able to reach across the distance to strike at her. Could she use the furniture for protection, or would he toss the flimsy metal desk at her? "If there is a problem, I am happy to handle it. If you give me the details ..." she offered.

"Do not play me, Geeth!" Sselmin-dor shouted. Such a display of venom was unusual for the First and he fought to control his voices. "I know what you did. All of it," he said as he held his tone to a reasonable level. "Come in," he ordered.

A shadowy figure moved in from the corridor and revealed itself to be Shurvil-maj, her usual teal-blue *chutar* leathers dull and creased and her red eyes clouded. She had the appearance of one who had not rested in some time. She bent her neck towards the First, but her eyes pointedly avoided Orval-geeth.

Geeth could think of only one reason for her presence and decided to confront it head-on rather than let the First retain the initiative. "Ah. This concerns the Seventh," she commented as if discussing the climate. "I understand a message was received at Mid-port."

Those words drew anger from the Voice of the Seventh. "Do not pretend. I know you read that message. You know exactly what happened … because you arranged the whole thing!"

The Eyes of the First turned to her principal, her arms held out in dismay. "I'm sorry. I don't know what all this is about."

It was difficult to say who was angrier at that response, the First or Shurvil-maj. But Maj kept her thoughts to herself while Sselmindor answered coldly, "The lies end; the deceit ends. Now!" He walked slowly around the desk that separated them, stopping at the far corner and effectively blocking Geeth's escape on that side. "I know about the actions you took. The transactions I never approved; the payments. Trading away the treasure of the band for your own needs."

Orval-geeth ducked her head. "I act only to relieve you of the tedious burdens of your office, to allow you to focus on more important issues," she deflected.

"You are Eyes of the First, not my Voice as Shurvil-maj was to the Seventh," Dor countered. "You do not have the power to act in my name!"

She bent her neck low, looking up with trepidation. "Then I was in error. I acted only as I believed you would on certain minor items." Raising her head slightly she tried again to explain away whatever the First had found. "I thought it was what you wanted as First. I did the same for Leeyak-dar when I served him."

"You dare speak his name," Shurvil-maj hissed from across the desk.

For a second Geeth thought the female might attack her. It was common knowledge across the All-Band: males fought to exhaust their opponent; females fought to disfigure. At that moment, she decided she had more to fear from Maj than Dor. Still, where she might have to cower before the First, she refused to bend the neck to a lesser lieutenant. Orval-geeth drew herself up and reminded them both, "I served Leeyak-dar for more than nine orbits. I regret his loss as much as you."

"Liar!" Maj exploded. "You murdered him!"

"A strong accusation. Do you have any proof to your claim?" Geeth demanded while sneering at the other female.

"Yes," Sselmin-dor answered dryly, wondering if Geeth had forgotten he was there. "When Shurvil-maj first brought her suspicions to me, I thought it was simple jealousy. But there were too many instances; too many connections that could not be explained. The payments you made for information I never saw. For slaves that were never delivered to our holding pens. Payments to Uhl-reej for ores and gases we never received; for things that band doesn't even produce!" He snapped his jaw in anger. "Did you think we were all fools? That we would not trace your dealings." He looked to Shurvil-maj.

The Voice of the late Seventh was calmer as she pecked at a dataplate. "You worked hard at covering your tracks," she commented as a claw slid across the screen. "At least, for an amateur. It was difficult to follow the incomplete information provided by so many within Shad-var back to the source, but eventually a pattern formed. The agents you sent to Garr-sum were not as careful, and the female here that worked with them was no better. This time, it was easy to connect the points, and they all led back to you." Maj took a deep breath. "I wondered why Hymrek-po brought his offer to me rather than someone higher up. Shad-var had no trades with his band for orbits; he had no reason to even know of me."

Orval-geeth offered no words, so Maj continued. "But the strangest part was what he offered to sell. Information and slaves that Uhl-reej could never hope to possess. Information that was strangely similar, indeed, nearly identical to what *Diamond Point* captured for Shad-var last-orbit. And how odd that the *hooman* slave we captured who provided all this information cannot be found now." She stared at Geeth, wondering if anything could shame her. "Did Hymrek-po know that he was selling our own information back to us?"

Orval-geeth's stance made it clear she was not impressed by the younger female's diatribe. "I don't know about any of this," she said with distain, then looked to the First. "I have served you for four orbits. Can you truly believe the speculations of this newcomer? She is just trying to hide the fact that she brought bad information to her commander." Turning back to Maj, "We have only her word that payments were made to this other band. It is more likely that the treasure is now hidden in Shurvil-maj's private vault!"

Sselmin-dor was unmoved. "Again, your agents betray you. Too many of the raids *Dominator* made were based on information that came from you. Information changed to hide the dangers that any sane commander would avoid. But this last raid ... this time, you hid the fact that the information was useless. It was impossible to take any ship from the *hooman* waste-zone. You guaranteed not just their failure, but their deaths."

"If the Seventh made flawed choices, the fault is his. That is not my doing," Geeth insisted as she looked for a way to drive a wedge between the First and vile Maj. He needed to see her as an inferior copy looking to steal Geeth's place in the band.

Sselmin-dor ignored her rantings. "But the worst part was your reason for such betrayal. We know why you did all this; why you spent orbits on your plan. Why you stole treasure from your band. You plotted against us. You would have destroyed *Dominator* and because of your tricks eleven members of Shad-var will never again contribute to the band." The sneer returned to his snout. "You betrayed us for your sick, perverted belief in ... family," he accused, spitting out the final word as if it were filth.

"Orval-brak, your egg-mate," Shurvil-maj added. "All this began after he failed on his last raid."

"Never speak his name," Orval-geeth hissed as she slammed the desktop, leaving deep bends in the thin metal. "He did not fail; he was betrayed by your vaunted Seventh!"

"He failed!" Sselmin-dor repeated. "*Silver Bounty* bore the scars of that fight. They could not wait for him forever."

"You weren't there!" Geeth screamed. "Brak never failed. He was twice the male either you or that pathetic Leeyak-dar ever were."

"Enough!" Sselmin-dor roared. "You stole from the band. You killed our kind. All for your perversion. You are not just an aberration; you are an abomination. If it were up to me, you would be ended as you ended the others, in the dead of space. But the Chief chose to spare you."

Orval-geeth held her head high. "Because he knows the value I bring to the band."

The First snorted. "Because killing you would make your crimes public, and bring shame to Shad-var. He thinks of the band. Not you," he countered. The sneer grew. "But I have found a suitable punishment."

Sselmin-dor pressed a button on his collar and a trio of enforcers rushed into the room, shock-rods at the ready. The larger male roughly attached shackles to Orval-geeth's arms, binding them to her sides.

The First snapped his jaw twice. "Orval-geeth, you wish to wallow in your depravity like an Ooverg. Then you will serve Shad-var like an Ooverg. You will be taken to the foundry on Barem where you will work the mines and feed the furnace, as any other Ooverg would. Your name is removed. You are no longer a member of Shad-var; you are property. You are Shad-var 56137." He waved an arm, and the enforcers pulled their prisoner towards the door. "See that the leathers and adornments are returned to my office."

As they dragged her away, Orval-geeth howled. "You cannot hurt me! I defeated you. All of you. The great principals of Shad-var – you think you know everything. But I was smarter than you. I beat you, and you can never change that. Never! You are nothing! Remember that!"

When the newly minted slave's voice finally faded away down the corridor, Shurvil-maj turned to the First. "How long do you think she will last there?"

Sselmin-dor's heavy brow shielded his eyes. "You know how quickly we go through slaves on Barem. Of course, I expect she'll be leading a slave revolt within a nine-mark or two," he half joked. When the amusement fell from his eyes, he added, "Then the slave-master can kill her when he puts down the revolt, along with every slave foolish enough to follow her."

Maj shook her head in approval, then turned the discussion to more important matters. "Who will be the new Seventh? Who do I serve now?" With a tilt to her head, she asked, "Will it be the Ninth?"

Sselmin-dor gurgled at the thought. "The Ninth? Rolehn-dru will be lucky to keep the position he has now that his protector is gone. And the Eighth is only slightly less useless than Dru. No, the Chief will name a new Seventh in time. Until then, I expect you to continue to serve as Voice of the Seventh, reporting to me." He eyed her slowly, as if inspecting a crate before taking delivery. "After that, we will find other tasks for you. You have proven yourself useful."

"It will be as you say, First," Maj replied, ducking her head to the side and moving closer to the First. Her breathing changed, becoming deep and throaty as the distance between them diminished. She heard his breathing begin to match her own.

Sselmin-dor was distracted for a long moment but recovered. "Yes. Good. Well ... I will return to my office. Without my Eyes, there is much I must handle myself now." After squeezing past Shurvil-maj, he hurried from the room without a look back.

Maj flicked her tongue, picking up the scent of the retreating First. Satisfied, she looked around the room, stopping at the large window behind the desk that looked out onto the waters of the bay below. *Yes. This will do very nicely*, she thought. *A new desk; some new moss. I'll be able to accomplish much more here. Much more.*

ACKNOWLEDGEMENTS

As with the previous entry in the *Tales of the Solar Commonwealth*, I decided this was the perfect time to revisit one of the novels of the Solar Commonwealth saga ('saga' sounds so much more grandiose than 'meandering series of barely related stories').

This story was planned all along to be a follow up to **The Draconis Campaign**, especially when I realized how long that novel was already. It gives me a chance to change the novella's point of view and focus on the aliens rather than the humans. Now we have a chance to see the galaxy from the Krayd perspective. This is a technique done to great effect by Alan Dean Forster in his Humanx Commonwealth series and I thought I would try my hand at it. I leave it to you, the readers, to determine how well (or badly) I acquitted myself.

The scenes featuring Terrans are there largely to connect this tale to the Solar Commonwealth series; the cameo appearance by the Regent is a contractual obligation. The Ssenn imparted great powers to the leader of humanity, including the right of script approval. After all, it's his universe and we are only his guests.

As ever, I must thank my wife Kate for serving as both my proofreader and my editor. Without her, none of these books would be written. If you have any complaints after reading this tome, please address those complaints to her.

My son, James, continues to review my work, pointing out my mistakes and making sure I don't accidently contradict the future I already covered in earlier works. My daughter Erin and her husband, Shane, are a little behind in their reading. I have to say, I was surprised that my new son-in-law was not a voracious reader of sci-fi. I'm starting to question this latest generation of engineers. Where's their devotion to the future?!

Once again, I thank all those around the globe who have written reviews of the previous books. There is nothing better than seeing when something you created is enjoyed by another. I hope that after reading this episode, you will take the time to drop a note with your thoughts – good, bad or other. All are welcome … but of course good reviews are preferred.

MAIN CHARACTERS

Krayd

Shad-var Band:

Leeyak-dar – Seventh of Shad-var.

Sselmin-dor – First of Shad-var.

Orval-geeth – Eyes of the First.

Shurvil-maj – Voice of the Seventh.

Telrin-vak – Master; Swift Raider *Dominator*.

Choban-hath – Overseer; Swift Raider *Dominator*.

Naymur-elv – Steerer; Swift Raider *Dominator*. Prize-master; *Emerald Dagger*.

Kalgun-dev – Raid-master; Swift Raider *Dominator, Emerald Dagger*.

Elldor-min – Drive-master; Swift Raider *Dominator, Emerald Dagger*.

Mayvel-Ahn – Crafter; Swift Raider *Dominator, Emerald Dagger*.

Uhl-reej Band:

Hymrek-po – Ear of the Third.

Terrans

Regent – Prime Executive; head of state of the Solar Commonwealth.

Erica Aliyah Hudson – Fleet Admiral; Commander-in-Chief of Solar Defense Forces.

Derya Hekmat – Commander; commanding officer, destroyer *Buenos Aires*.

Mayasawati (Joko) – Lieutenant Commander; executive officer, destroyer *Buenos Aires*.

Sam Midthunder – Lieutenant; commanding officer, gunboat *Brookhaven*.

Beren Özdemir – Ensign; executive officer, gunboat *Brookhaven*.

GLOSSARY

chutar – Kray-ssass. A livestock animal favored for its meat; its hide is often used by the second tier ranks of Krayd bands. It is frequently given a greyish-blue finish when worn by deputies of the first tier.

first-dark – English. Translation of the Kray-ssass term for 'sunset'.

first-light – English. Translation of the Kray-ssass term for 'sunrise'.

garm-liktee – Kray-ssass. Unit of time equal to one-eighteenth rotation of Kray-da; approx. 80 minutes.

garm-maltee – Kray-ssass. Unit of time equal to one-eighteenth *garm-liktee*; approx. 4 minutes, 26 seconds.

garm-voshtee – Kray-ssass. Unit of time equal to one-eighteenth *garm-maltee*; approx. 14.8 seconds.

gellrehk – Kray-ssass. Cheap, orange-tinted leather; normally used by the third tier ranks of Krayd bands.

hooman – Kray-ssass. The Krayd pronunciation of "human." It used by the Krayd to refer to both Tyndal and Terran as they cannot tell the two species apart.

last-mark – English. Translation of the Kray-ssass term for 'yesterday'.

mid-dark – English. Translation of the Kray-ssass term for 'midnight'.

mid-light – English. Translation of the Kray-ssass term for 'noon'.

muhlat – Kray-ssass. A hard-wood tree native to Kray-da; used for furniture as well as traditional weapons.

new-dark – English. Translation of the Kray-ssass term for 'evening'.

new-light – English. Translation of the Kray-ssass term for 'morning'.

next-mark – English. Translation of the Kray-ssass term for 'tomorrow'.

nine-mark – English. Nine rotation period. Krayd equivalent of a week.

orbit – English. Translation of the Kray-ssass term for 'year'.

over-dark – English. Translation of the Kray-ssass term for 'overnight'.

peevak – Kray-ssass. A derogatory term, possibly an expletive.

pleegot – Kray-ssass. A long, blue-green grass native to Kray-da. The pliable yet rugged material is often used in domiciles and offices to cover floors, walls and assorted furniture.

poondaz – Kray-ssass. A small mammal native to the southern continents on Kray-da; when threatened it burrows into the ground to hide from predators.

post-mid-light – English. Translation of the Kray-ssass term for 'afternoon'.

rotation – English. Translation of the Kray-ssass term for 'day'.

this-mark – English. Translation of the Kray-ssass term for 'today'.

triknar – Kray-ssass. A riding beast prized for its agility and endurance; its hide is favored by the upper ranks of Krayd bands.

zel-hosh – Kray-ssass. Unit of length equal to the average distance of a Kray-da (the home planet) to Hosh (the Krayd sun); approx. 1.046 AU or 156.47 Gm.

zel-kray – Kray-ssass. Unit of length equal to the average height of a Krayd male; approx. 1.62 meters.

ABOUT THE AUTHOR

John Lallier is author of the Solar Commonwealth series. He is a veteran of the software industry with a lifelong passion for science fiction – from the works of Asimov, Clarke and Bova, through the universes of Star Trek, Battlestar Galactica, Stargate, The Expanse and Star Carrier and so many others. After years of creating software for millions, he is now creating a universe for dozens. OK, really just for himself, but you are all welcome to come along for the ride.

You are all invited to pull up a chair and bring your own mug of coffee or tea (Earl Grey, hot of course; *raktajino* not available in all locations) and tour the worlds of the Commonwealth. If you find yourself enjoying the journey, you can find more at www.jclpress.com.

John lives in New York with his wife and two dogs. Fortunately, the treacherous cats have departed the house with his daughter, while she continues to ignore his warnings of their dastardly plot to dominate the galaxy. After all, the Feorae are based on somebody. . But who are the Krayd based on? An excellent question ... stay tuned for the big reveal.

www.ingramcontent.com/pod-product-compliance
Lightning Source LLC
Chambersburg PA
CBHW021158160726
47994CB00001B/269